I0591808

I Wanna Fucking Tear You Apart

by Morgan Gould

ıl SAMUEL FRENCH lı

FOR PRODUCTION INQUIRIES

UNITED STATES AND CANADA
info@concordtheatricals.com
1-866-979-0447

UNITED KINGDOM AND EUROPE
licensing@concordtheatricals.co.uk
020-7054-7298

Each title is subject to availability from Concord Theatricals Corp., depending upon country of performance. Please be aware that *I WANNA FUCKING TEAR YOU APART* may not be licensed by Concord Theatricals Corp. in your territory. Professional and amateur producers should contact the nearest Concord Theatricals Corp. office or licensing partner to verify availability.

This work is published by Samuel French, an imprint of Concord Theatricals Corp.

MUSIC AND THIRD-PARTY MATERIALS USE NOTE

IMPORTANT BILLING AND CREDIT REQUIREMENTS

I WANNA FUCKING TEAR YOU APART was first produced by Studio Theatre, Washington, DC, in 2017 with David Muse as Artistic Director and Meridith Burkus as Managing Director. The performance was directed by Morgan Gould and assistant directed by Laura Scialdone, with dramaturgy by Adrien-Alice Hansel, sets by Luciana Stecconi, costumes by Ivania Stack, lighting design by Andrew Cissna, and sound design by Justin Schmitz. The Production Stage Manager was Elizabeth Ribar, and the Assistant Stage Manager was Diane Schramke. The cast was as follows:

SAMANTHA (SAM) . . . . Nicole Spiezio

LEO . . . . Tommy Heleringer

CHLOE . . . . Anna O'Donoghue

I WANNA FUCKING TEAR YOU APART received developmental support through the 2016 Beatrice Terry Residency Program of The Drama League of New York, Roger T. Danforth, Artistic Director, Gabriel Shanks, Executive Director.

Additional development support was provided by Lark Play Development Center, SPACE on Ryder Farm, and Brooklyn College MFA Playwrights Workshop.

CHARACTERS

SAMANTHA (SAM) – Thirty-ish

LEO – Thirty-ish

CHLOE – Twenty-four or something disgusting

MIKE – Thirty-ish, HOT, any race. He can be played by a crew member, offstage as a voiceover, or even as a special guest star with a different fun performer who is put in each night... The point is to underline that Sam (like MANY fat women!) has a boyfriend. She is not alone or single. Have fun with it!

AUTHOR'S NOTES

No tricks from here on out. I promise.

All the transitions should be quick QUICK QUICK (unless otherwise indicated towards the end of the play or at the very beginning). I recommend that they mostly remain onstage during transitions. This way it feels like snapshots or a flipbook of the year. And before you ask, yes, I have thought about costume changes and tracking. It's all doable to make the scenes change very quickly. Don't have Sam change her pants that much. Have her pull a sweatshirt from under a couch cushion. Have her grab a robe from a hook. She does NOT need to exit and change her clothes every time. I've also built in a few places where Leo enters first so Sam can switch for seasons, etc. I won't micromanage, but just to say, don't add real estate for costume changes! It'll kill the momentum.

Bolded text is projected (don't worry, relax, it's just the titles of the months and a short sequence at the beginning).

Sam and Chloe were originally written to be played by white actors. While I completely support actors of the global majority playing the roles (I've seen a Latinx Sam and an Asian-American Chloe and it was great!), please be aware that the microaggressions in the play live in relation to their whiteness. Leo has been played by actors of different races, so be sure to consider how the final scenes (especially pages 73-74) where Sam confronts Leo may come off depending on his race relative to Sam's. Alternate text for Leo in **January** is provided for use at the back of the Acting Edition if you have an actor of color playing Leo. Use of the alternate scene is not required. The line that can be changed to accommodate the race or ethnicity of the actor playing Leo is noted in the alternate scene. Please contact Concord Theatricals for approval of any other changes, including dialogue changes for Sam and Chloe.

"Why does everyone always have a quote on a blank page before their play? I'm actually asking." – Anonymous

For Peter, thank you for being my soulmate, my brother, my truest love and

For Amir, thank you for being my muse, my partner, and the one who reminded me that no matter what, all my plays will be fat

You vast, brilliant unknowable creatures. I owe you both my life.

Prologue

(There is suddenly a blackout.)

(Projected text and voiceover of a gay, gay man:)

WELCOME TO [NAME OF THEATER OR VENUE]. TURN YOUR CELL PHONES OFF...

...YOU FILTHY ANIMALS.

(A song in the style of She Wants Revenge's "I Wanna Fucking Tear You Apart" starts playing.*)

(The projected text fades.)

(Before the lyric drops, a special bumps on [on the beat]. A man enters and stands in the spotlight. This is **LEO**. *He is in high drag. I don't totally know what that means. I think it's like, red and black and glitter and fabulous and sexy and queer.)*

---

* A license to produce the play *I Wanna Fucking Tear You Apart* does not include a performance license for the song "I Wanna Fucking Tear You Apart." The publisher and author suggest that the licensee contact ASCAP or BMI to ascertain the music publisher and contact such music publisher to license or acquire permission for performance of the song. If a license or permission is unattainable for "I Wanna Fucking Tear You Apart," the licensee may not use the song in the play *I Wanna Fucking Tear You Apart* but should create an original composition in a similar style or use a similar song in the public domain. For further information, please see the Music and Third-Party Materials Use Note on page iii.

(A fat woman enters. This is **SAM**. *She, too is in sexy, almost vampiric high drag.)*

(The whole next section is choreographic. It's not a dance, really. But it is moves on a beat, staging that syncs up with the rhythm of the song. Maybe it's a little runway-esque, high fashion. There is strutting. There is posing. It's sexy-funny-lazy.)

(The characters exit off to places. Blackout. The song keeps playing. Projected text appears, with the credits of the production. Everyone. Like in movies from the 90s. Like all the credits play before the movie. Like First Wives Club *and* My Best Friend's Wedding*.)*

(It occurs to me that this would be a logical place for a costume change. You should use the whole song, please. When it's over:)

(Suddenly, the lights bump up and we're in Leo and Sam's apartment. The whole play will take place here.)

(And don't worry. Despite this small musical interlude, this is a normal play.)

January

(**SAM** *enters, struggling with her keys. She is bundled up holding a brown paper bag. A TV show like* Sex and the City *blares from the TV.** *She slams the door. She looks at* **LEO**. *She has an announcement.*)

SAM. I've been thinking it must be hard to be a man.

LEO. It's not.

SAM. But when you go to the bathroom. Don't you have to decide? Don't you have to be like, "I'm peeing" or "I'm pooping"?

LEO. What?

SAM. Like you have to decide whether to stand or sit.

LEO. (*Still looking through the food.*) Gross. I don't like these woman conversations.

SAM. I get to decide in the moment. Right then. Which one. You know if I want to pee or –

LEO. (*Stopping, turning to face her. Serious.*) I don't like bathroom things. I don't like bathroom humor or discussions. Please stop.

SAM. You should be more appreciative of my inquisitive nature.

(**LEO** *opens a box of the food.*)

LEO. Sesame chicken is for me?

SAM. Yes. And the brown rice.

---

* A license to produce *I Wanna Fucking Tear You Apart* does not include a performance license for any Third Party or copyrighted recordings or images. Licensees must acquire rights for any copyrighted recordings or images or create their own.

LEO. Wow.

SAM. You're surprised I knew what to get you?

LEO. I didn't know if you had the brown rice memo or not.

SAM. You switched to brown last month.

LEO. Right. But I didn't know you knew.

> (*Getting up,* **SAM** *crosses to the kitchen, starts washing her hands.*)

SAM. (*Calling from off.*) I know all, I see all.

> (*She reenters then tosses him a Diet Coke. Only Coke. Never Pepsi!!!!**)

> (*He catches it and cracks it. She exits again, brings out two plates. Sits down in front of the couch on the floor. He joins her. She plates his food for him as he watches and does nothing to help. She picks off a hot pepper. Slides his plate to him. He waits patiently while she plates her own. He still doesn't help.*)

LEO. How much do I owe you?

SAM. Nothing, don't worry about it.

LEO. (*Not super convincing.*) No. Come on, you always pay.

SAM. And you always let me, that's part of your charm.

> (*Tiny pause.* **LEO** *attempts a small standoff.*)

LEO. (*Breaking into a cheesy grin.*) It is isn't it?

> (*He takes a giant bite, then, with mouth full...*)

Oh! Guess what happened to me on my lunch break today.

---

* A license to produce *I Wanna Fucking Tear You Apart* does not include a license to publicly display any branded logos or trademarked images. Licensees must acquire rights for any logos and/or images or create their own.

SAM. What?

>   *(They start to eat.*)*

LEO. I solved the Israeli-Palestinian crisis.

SAM. ...go on.

LEO. Well, you know how like, everyone has been trying to think of a way to fix that?

SAM. I do. I. Um. Do.

LEO. Well, I know this sounds nuts, but like. I figured it out.

SAM. Please. Enlighten me.

LEO. You're being snide. I can tell you're being snide.

SAM. It's just. You know. The greatest political minds of our time...and like, the past thousand years couldn't figure this out. But one visit to Pret A Manger and you've come up with it? Forgive my small doubt.

LEO. Okay, but you have to admit I'm pretty political. I'm up on politics. You've even said so.

SAM. I know. I'm not disputing that.

LEO. Seriously though. Remember when I explained Edward Snowden to you?

SAM. Yes.

LEO. So like. It's not totally out there that I could actually have the solution.

SAM. Okay, okay. I'm all ears. Lay it on me.

LEO. Okay so the big issue is the West Bank. So I say. We take it over...

SAM. Who is we? The US?

---

* This next section through the middle of page 7 was written for a white actor. There is alternate text available for an actor of color playing **LEO** included at the end of this script. If you would like to cast someone outside those races, please contact Concord Theatricals for alternate text.

LEO. Yeah. Or like, you know, NATO. The UN.

SAM. *(A smirk.)*...Right okay. Go on.

LEO. We take it over and we are just like, "everyone out."

SAM. Mmmhmmm.

LEO. And then like, after like, the Palestinians behave themselves we can give it back to them.

SAM. The Palestinians behave themselves?

LEO. Yeah. Like, once they get organized and stop bombing us –

SAM. Bombing Israel, you mean.

LEO. Well yeah, but like, you know like I still have tons of family there –

SAM. Oh I know.

LEO. So yeah, once they calm down, we give it back.

SAM. Okay. So who defines what "calm down" means?

LEO. The US.

SAM. Okay. Fine. So let's say that magically Palestine goes for this idea...

LEO. I mean why wouldn't they? They want the violence to stop too –

SAM. Sure, okay. But then. What about all the Israelis who just bought like, condos / or whatever?

LEO. Settlements. / They're called settlements.

SAM. Fine, those settlements? That weren't supposed to be there? What? Do they just get kicked out of their expensive houses?

LEO. Yeah.

SAM. But like, if you just bought a house, you'd be like HELL NO.

LEO. Yeah, but the Israeli government should make them.

SAM. Well if they were willing to do that there would have been no settlements in the first place.

LEO. Right.

SAM. So. I kind of think that your solution works in theory, but in practice. In practice it might have some flaws.

LEO. Well, I mean I only thought about it for like fifteen minutes.

SAM. Sure.

LEO. But like, I think the basis for my logic was pretty good.

SAM. No it was. It was.

LEO. Yeah.

(Pause. He checks his phone.)

Any word on if Emily's boyfriend is gay?

SAM. They're married now. It's her husband.

LEO. Right. Any word?

SAM. Word from where? Where would this word come from?

LEO. I think he is.

SAM. *(Taking a bite.)* Me too. He's like the world's most quintessential bear. He fucking owns Crocs.

LEO. Yeah, but, more like a bear/otter borderline with a hint of / Muscle Mary.

> (**SAM** *cuts in with a really loud, sustained scream.*)

SAM. / AHHHHHHHHHHHHHHH

LEO. / Oh my god, / what?

SAM. / HOT PEPPER HELPPPPPPPPPPP

> (**LEO** *freaks out, he gets up, runs around the kitchen.*)

> (*Still screaming and freaking out for real.*) THIS IS THE WORST PAIN I'VE EVER KNOWN.

> (**LEO** *finds a bag of Tostitos. He grabs a chip and begins rubbing on* **SAM**'s *tongue frantically.*)

LEO. (*Sincere.*) CALM DOWN

SAM. Oh god oh god oh god...wait. That's actually working.

LEO. I mean. I thought, like, it's like bread?

SAM. (*Discovering.*) I'm okay.

> (*They pause. Then...*)

Oh, also I had a really funny idea for a chapter of the book.

LEO. What?

SAM. It's a series – like, it's like, every so often I deviate from the narrative and like, there's just, a food diary.

LEO. A food diary?

SAM. Yeah, just like everything she ate. Funny?

LEO. Could be. If the things she ate...are funny.

SAM. They would be like – they'd be like, normal. And then there would be like "box of cookies."

LEO. I don't get it yet.

SAM. No, I promise. It's funny.

LEO. Okay.

SAM. Like it would be like, "kale, arugula, carrots, moo goo gai pan."

LEO. Maybe if you wrote it out...

SAM. I don't know if those are the real ones. I just mean like, I like the idea of deviation. Like a random narrative DEVIATION, you know?

LEO. Yeah. Okay. Yeah, I get what you mean. What if it was like. What if it was...a to-do list. Instead of a food diary.

SAM. Ooo. Maybe. / Hm. I like that. To-do list.

LEO. Yeah like "gym, buy zit cream, / mani-pedi" or something...yeah.

SAM. Call gyno!

LEO. *(A tinge grossed out.)* ...sure.

SAM. Shop the sales rack at Loehmann's /

LEO. LOEHMANN'S! I LOVE / LOEHMANN'S, "Baby, you wanna go to Loehmann's?"

SAM. LOEHMANNNN'SSSSSS / I can get anything at Loehman's oh god oh god LOEHMAN'S /

LEO. Ferns, chairs, / couches / a hat, a sweater –

SAM. I WANNA BUY DRESSES / AT LOEHMANN'S

LEO. DRESSSSSSSSESSSSS!!!!

SAM. A MINI A MAXI I CAN'T CHOOSE

LEO & SAM. *(Chanting.)* LOEHMANN'S LOEHMANN'S LOEHMANN'S LOEHMANN'S

LEO. Let's get WAXES! We'll be hairless at LOEHMANN'S!

(He starts to hump her, she faux orgasms.)

*(**LEO** gets a text. They immediately stop. **SAM** sips the Diet Coke. He checks his phone.)*

LEO. You know what would be fun? Hearing Josh's band play next Friday.

SAM. Uhhhh... Yeah. I'll check my calendar. But also, where is it?

LEO. Bush / wick.

SAM. / BUSHWICK? I don't go to Bushwick for ANYONE. Remember the time I got that admin job in Bushwick and I went once and then told them I was going out to buy Post-Its and I just never came back? I just couldn't. I just couldn't.

LEO. Come on. It'll be fun! It is often extremely fun when we get there! AND you know we'll take cabs / both ways and then complain about being broke for the rest of our lives. / We've been doing this since we were freshmen in college.

SAM. / Ubers. How dare you...

　　　　(A pause.)

LEO. I feel like you still kind of don't like him.

SAM. What? I totally like Josh. Josh is fine.

LEO. Fine?

SAM. Yeah, he's. Josh is cool. He has a keen Facebook presence. I've never said I didn't like him. I've never said that.

　　　　(Pause.)

LEO. Hmm. Maybe I'll try to get him to meet me in Manhattan / on Thursday.

SAM. / LEO, IT'S 9:03. / You had one job.

　　　　*(**LEO** scrambles around looking for the remote.)*

LEO. Fuck. I know. / I'm panicking.

SAM. Hurry, we can't miss the beginning of Quickfire / or we won't understand the rules.

> *(We hear a theme song of a culinary show opening.* They eat in silence. Then with the show, they both say the words in bold:)*

VOICEOVER.

> Ten Chefs are still alive to go head to head in the **definitive culinary battle**

> Awarded to the champion:

> **Two hundred and fifty thousand dollars** furnished by **Hidden Valley Ranch**

> Along with a spread in ***Bon Appétit* Magazine**

> An appearance at Le Petit Gourmet Festival **in scenic Charleston**

> A **massively generous kitchen set** from MoMA design

VOICEOVER.

> A headlining slot at **the Anderson Lumiere Food Theater at Horse Head in Napa Valley**

> And the coveted title of **BEST CHEF!**

LEO. What's worse: the season where that cute guy Sam got eliminated for his banh mi or Sandra Oh leaving *Grey's Anatomy*?

SAM. Obviously Sandra Oh. / Obviously.

---

* A license to produce *I Wanna Fucking Tear You Apart* does not include a performance license for any third-party or copyrighted recordings or images. Licensees must acquire rights for any copyrighted recordings or images or create their own.

LEO. / No, I know, of course. No. I wasted a question.

SAM. I mean I'll watch it forever, but I will still always recognize the show is completely and fundamentally nothing now / that she's gone.

LEO. God, that show is so groundbreaking. / Why don't people understand?

SAM. Yeah I mean, ultimately, it's a show about female friendship. Ultimately? That's what it's about.

> (*They eat. The show plays. After a minute or two.*)

Ooh, sudden-death Quick / fire.

LEO. / Can I admit something to you?

SAM. Always.

LEO. It's annoying.

SAM. I would expect nothing less.

LEO. I had.

I had a reaction the other day.

When you were talking about Gary.

SAM. HIV Gary?

LEO. Yeah.

SAM. ...What?

LEO. It's just like. I feel like you were kind of judgmental about it.

SAM. I mean. I'm not judgmental that he has HIV, I'm just like. I wouldn't sleep with someone I knew had it. I know that's not like "PC" or open-minded. And seriously. I don't judge anyone who has it, but I wouldn't do it. Mostly because I just like, wouldn't be able to like GET OFF. Because I wouldn't be able to concentrate because I'd be worried I would get AIDS.

LEO. HIV.

SAM. That's what I meant.

LEO. Just. You should be correct about it.

SAM. Whatever, you're the worst misogynist / I know so don't get all pissy with me about HIV.

LEO. Allllllright here we go again...

I'm not pissy! I was just confessing I had a reaction, that's all. And like, I just. I feel like normally you and I agree on these topics. And like, when you are mean and judgey about gay stuff, I always weirdly take it sort of personally because I just know that could be me you're talking about. And honestly, this is why I didn't tell you about the poppers last Christmas Eve.

SAM. Well poppers are fine, I would never judge POPPERS.

LEO. I know you wouldn't. But I just. On these things, I need you to be on my side. Team fat/gay.

> *(He accidentally points to her as he says "gay" and himself as he says "fat," laughs, and reverses it. She laughs a little too. It's a weird tiny accident.)*

Team gay/fat. I'm gay. You're fat.

SAM. But I have a pretty face. *(Pause.)* So fuck, was I being like, weird and homophobic-y?

LEO. Yes! And you said it in front of Steven and Jeff. And I think Steven might be positive.

SAM. No!

LEO. I mean, I don't know for sure but...

SAM. Oh my god, really? / Fuck. That's so embarrassing. If he's positive, I sounded like a total dick!

LEO. / Yes!

You sounded like a total dick either way.

(From the TV we hear, "Coming up..." **SAM**
and **LEO** *cover their ears and say, "La la la la
la" until the teaser ends.)*

SAM. Wait so should I do something? Should I message
/ Steven?

LEO. / God no! / Oh my god!

SAM. / No, you're right, that would be awful.

LEO. Yeah, let it go, just don't be such a judgmental bitch
next time.

SAM. I can't make any promises.

LEO. Believe me, I know.

(They eat in comfortable silence, watching TV.)

So. Question for you.

SAM. What's up?

LEO. Totally fine to say no.

SAM. I know.

LEO. What's your money sitch like at the moment?

SAM. How much do you need?

LEO. Well. It depends. Like. I'm overdrawn –

SAM. Fuck. I hate that.

LEO. Yeah. So either a hundred dollars, which would take
me out of the red. Or like, seven hundred dollars. Like.
If you want, with seven hundred dollars I could pay
you my part of the rent and that would be a BIG relief
for both of us. But I know that's a lot. Totally say no if
you want.

SAM. Woof. That's like twenty hours of grantwriting,
dude. When can you pay it back?

LEO. One hundred dollars I could pay back in four days. Seven hundred dollars I could pay back on the thirty-first.

SAM. Can you still do one hundred dollars in four days and then the six hundred dollars on the thirty-first?

LEO. Yes. But I mean, only if helps you. I know you said you like loaning because then you don't spend it in the meantime. Like, if you give it to me, you can't spend it before the rent is due.

SAM. True. Let me check my balance.

(*Long silence while she checks. He eats.*)

Hmm.

LEO. No is totally okay.

SAM. No. No. I can do the seven hundred dollars.

LEO. Really? Oh my god, really?

SAM. I just. You HAVE to pay me the WHOLE thing on the thirty-first. I'm going to Providence to Lauren's bridal shower.

LEO. Gross.

SAM. Yeah. And the Maid of Honor's in AA, so there's not even drinking.

LEO. That's irresponsible.

SAM. I know. Anyway, I need it in cash by like noon. For real. Like REALLY, Leo.

LEO. Got it. My check gets dropped into my account late late late Thursday night, so Friday morning, I'll get up before work and go to the ATM and get you cash.

SAM. Cool. Then yeah. Yeah. I can do seven hundred dollars. Here...

(*She types a bit. His phone beeps.*)

Just Venmo'd.

LEO. *(Disappointed.)* Oh.

SAM. What? No?

LEO. I just... I kind of wanted some now. Like can we go to the ATM?

SAM. Do an instant transfer.

LEO. Ooo. But I haaate giving that percentage away to a big corporation, so –

SAM. Literally Satan. But fine reject the Ven–

> *(The sound of chaos coming from the TV. We hear "put down your knives.")*

BOTH. Oh shit!!!!

> *(The following can all overlap:)*

SAM. Jesus! What a monster. He didn't even plate! He didn't even plate!

LEO. I can't believe it –

SAM. I cannot BELIEVE / he'd never used a pressure cooker.

LEO. EVERY. SEASON. EVERY. / FUCKING. SEASON.

SAM. / Literally, every single season. Like wouldn't you / STUDY how to use a pressure cooker if you got picked to be on the show?

LEO. Google it. Google it. Your mother literally has one. Or like, ask one of your line cooks.

SAM. Everyone across America has an Instapot. Go borrow one!

LEO. Hipsters have them. GO BORROW ONE!

SAM. That one hurts. It really does. He was so talented.

LEO. And here I am still REELING from Nicole going home for the tortellini / like NEVER MAKE PASTA GOD...And now this.

SAM. / Seriously so dumb of her – EXACTLY

> (**SAM** *has a really sad pause.* **LEO** *looks at his phone. A beat.*)

SAM. *(Re: the guy who just got kicked off.)* He will never get a James Beard Award now. Never.

> (*She looks to* **LEO** *for his response. He is engrossed in his phone.*)

SAM. Leo.

LEO. *(Snapping out of it, trying to fake he was listening.)* Oh...what? Yeah. James Beard. Sad. Very sad.

> (*He goes back to his phone. He types. Swipes. He shows her.*)

LEO. Is this a good profile pic?

SAM. Grindr or scruff?

LEO. Sniffies.

> (**SAM** *looks again.*)

SAM. *(Calm, casual, matter of fact.)* No.

LEO *(Sliiiiiightly but only slightly annoyed.)* Hm.

> (*He looks off into the distance, pondering.*)

> (*Lights.*)

February

(**SAM** *enters casually from her room. She opens the fridge to get a Diet Coke. She takes out a two liter, and it is empty. How dare Leo drink it all!!!*)

(*She goes to Leo's door and throws the empty bottle in.*)

LEO. *(From off.)* Ow! What the fuck?!

(**SAM** *storms off to her room passive-aggressively.* **LEO** *appears a second later. He looks around. She's gone. He sighs. He did drink all the Diet Coke after all. He grabs his keys as if to go get more, just as* **SAM** *reenters. He opens his mouth [perhaps to apologize] but then he spots her holding a Sharpie and a piece of paper and pointedly ignoring him.*)

(*She stalks past him and begins writing something on the paper. She posts a giant sign on the fridge that says "PLEASE REPLACE Diet Coke" as* **LEO** *pretends not to look. He is furious. Last time they fought they agreed no notes!*)

(*She finishes and walks past him without looking at him, flounces onto the couch. In a fit of silent rage,* **LEO** *rips down the note and crumples it, throwing it in the sink. He dumps dish soap on it and angrily grabs a spoon and jams it in the sink on the note, destroying it.* **SAM** *has meanwhile turned on the TV. She watches, pretending not to notice* **LEO**'s *antics. We hear a theme song like the one for* The Chilling Adventures of Sabrina *or anything currently airing that is spooky,* *horror-y, or murder-y.*[*] **SAM** *starts filing her nails without looking at him.)*

(When **LEO** *hears the show, he swallows his rage. He really wants to watch. After a moment or two,* **LEO** *carefully crosses, sitting on the opposite end of the couch.* **SAM** *still doesn't look at him, she files.* **LEO** *casts a glance* **SAM**'s *way. After several moments/ minutes/theater time-appropriate length,* **SAM** *hands him the nail file. He smiles to himself. He is about to file his nails when...)*

(Something violent happens on screen. They both make a face/gasp. Perhaps they grasp each other.)

(Lights.)

---

* A license to produce *I Wanna Fucking Tear You Apart* does not include a performance license for any third-party or copyrighted recordings or images. Licensees must acquire rights for any copyrighted recordings or images or create their own.

March

(**SAM** *sits playing Nintendo. Super Nintendo to be exact. Mario World or Donkey Kong. It's late. Like two a.m. She's involved. She eats a popsicle.* **LEO** *enters the kitchen.*)

(*He sighs.*)

(*Sounds of a video game being played.* **LEO** *waits for her to say more. She doesn't. She's too focused.* **LEO** *sighs more loudly, trying to get her attention. She keeps playing.*)

(**LEO** *sighs again. Even louder.*)

(*She glances at him, but clearly has a benchmark she's trying to hit on the level.*)

SAM. *(Missing something in the game.)* Fuck.

(*The following is a small deviation from his sighing...*)

LEO. You can just hop on the mushroom and it's actually the bouncy kind.

SAM. Really?

LEO. Yeah. Then you don't even need to worry about the shell.

SAM. Hm.

(*She does it. A video game victory sound plays.* *End of the level.* **SAM** *exhales.* **LEO** *hops over the back of the couch to sit next to*

---

* A license to produce I Wanna Fucking Tear You Apart does not include performance usage rights for any third-party or copyrighted video games. Licensees should create their own sound effects or use sound effects in the public domain.

her. He sighs again – back to him, after all!
Deviation over.)

SAM. *(Finally acknowledging him.)* So what's up?

LEO. *(Sighing.)* Nothing.

SAM. Quarter-life crisis again?

LEO. You know now that we're in our thirties, it's not really a quarter-life crisis anymore.

　　　*(****SAM**** gets up to get a snack.)*

SAM. *(From kitchen.)* Well I plan to live to be one hundred and twenty so for me it is.

LEO. Oh god. I want a bus to hit me like next year.

SAM. It's good to have goals.

　　　*(****SAM**** returns with pretzel crisps and a bowl.*
　　　*****LEO**** sticks his hand in. They start eating*
　　　them.*)

So why the sighing? For real.

LEO. It's dumb.

It's dumb and I'm sick of hearing myself.

I'm sick of forcing you to listen to my stupid whining.

I don't know how you tolerate me.

SAM. I tolerate you because you're the only person who tolerates me.

I tolerate you because I love you.

I tolerate you because I don't think of it as tolerating you because I enjoy your presence.

---

*Please note that it does not offend my sensibilities to imagine this scene with **LEO** and **SAM** passing a bowl between them. A word of caution: this should not be a funny stoner scene, or a scene about them smoking pot. And they should not be like "haha we're high." That's annoying. They are professional stoners. It doesn't alter them that much to smoke a bowl, just like drinking a beer barely registers to a regular drinker.

LEO. That doesn't speak very well to your taste.

SAM. This from a man who wears an orange puffy coat three months out of the year.

But now isn't time for petty squabbling.

Praytell, what's wrong?

LEO. I just feel like I'm wasting my life.

SAM. Oh this one again?

LEO. Yes.

SAM. Well, you are wasting your life.

LEO. SAM. You always minimize my struggles.

SAM. Come on, Leo! Aren't we all wasting our lives? We're WRITERS. We're not living life. We're stuck in rooms and cafes and bathrooms floors WRITING about life. We're the worst sort of fuckheads.

LEO. We're just self-aware fuckheads.

SAM. I don't know that many self-aware writers.

LEO. Fair.

(They chew. They smoke.)

SAM. Okay so. Do you want me to be comforting or do you want me to be honest?

LEO. Are they mutually exclusive?

SAM. They are right now.

LEO. *(Bracing himself a little.)* Honest.

*(**SAM** exhales a puff of weed smoke.)*

SAM. *(Turning to him.)* Leo. You know I think you're a genius.

LEO. So far this is bordering on comforting.

SAM. But –

>   (**SAM** *passes* **LEO** *the bowl.*)

LEO. Stop there.

SAM. *(Smiling.)* BUT. Leo. You don't do the work. And I know it's not because you can't. It's because you're afraid.

>   (**LEO** *exhales some smoke.*)

LEO. I know. I know.

>   (**SAM** *takes the bowl.*)

SAM. I know you know. But what can you do / about it?

LEO. UGH I don't know. How are you so motivated? How do you do it? How do you just...GO ON?

SAM. It's two a.m. and I'm playing Super Mario.

LEO. Yeah, but I bet you wrote today.

SAM. ...

LEO. You're the worst.

SAM. It's just. I make it a priority. In a way that. Seems... difficult...for you.

LEO. ...

SAM. It's just. You seem to find time to talk on the phone for hours, watch shows, jack off, go shopping, drink...

LEO. ...

SAM. I don't mean to sound judgy.

LEO. You do.

SAM. *(Turning to him.)* Look. Leo. I would never say anything to you about this if I didn't love you.

LEO. *(Mumbling.)* Yeah, I know you *love me.*

SAM. AND. I think

YOU.

ARE.

AMAZING.

I love you BECAUSE of how amazing you are.

You know I think that.

You know I couldn't be your best friend if I didn't think that.

You KNOW that.

You KNOW I couldn't stand to be friends with someone I thought was untalented.

LEO. I guess...

SAM. I BROKE UP WITH MY BOYFRIEND OF SEVEN YEARS WHEN HE MADE A BAD SHORT FILM

LEO. You were ALSO bored with him. You ALSO were bored.

SAM. YEAH BECAUSE HE MADE BAD FILMS AND DIDN'T KNOW THEY WERE BAD – THE HANDS! THE HANDS THAT MADE THOSE BAD FILMS! THEY TOUCHED ME! THEY TOUCHED ME!

      (**LEO** *smiles despite himself.*)

It's like his fingers are little bugs crawling all over me.

      (**SAM** *takes a hit of the bowl to cleanse herself. As she does so...*)

LEO. *(Using his index finger to be gross and creepy.)* The cock that was INSIDE YOU was attached to the MAN who had the HANDS who made the bad short film! MUAHAHAHAHAH

(**LEO** *creepily lunges at her pretending to be a giant penis. He wriggles around on her. She shrieks. He starts to gnaw on her.*)

NOM NOM NOM I AM MR. UNTALENTED PENIS I EAT BAD SHORT FILMS FOR BREAKFAST LUNCH AND DINNER

I WILL FEED ON YOUR TALENT

TO MAKE MY BAD SHORT FILMMMMSSSSSSS

SAM. *(Laugh-screaming.)* Leo! Ewwwwwww

EWWWWW

EEEEEEEEE

LEO. *(Sucking on her arm.)* I will suck out your SKILLZ

AND USE THEM TO ENTER MEDIOCRE FESTIVALLLLSSSSSSSSSS

WHERE MY BAD SHORT FILMS WILL

TRIUMPHHHHHHH

SAM. YOU ARE THE WORST AHHHHHH

(*Sam's bedroom door swings open. **MIKE** enters [or maybe he doesn't; see casting note in the beginning of the play], sleepy-eyed. He's wearing only boxers. He's hot. Like super hot. He might be a person of color. But most importantly, he is really hot and wearing boxers. He has cute glasses on. Slippers.*)

MIKE. *(Bleary-eyed.)* Sam? Everything okay?

LEO. Hey, dude.

SAM. Sorry, babe. Didn't mean to wake you up.

MIKE. *(Smiling a little, still waking up.)* You two are psychos.

LEO. We prefer "selectively deviant."

SAM. *(To* **LEO.***)* You stole that phrase from *Fifty Shades of Grey*, thief.

MIKE. *(To* **SAM.***)* You comin'?

SAM. In a minute, I promise.

> (**MIKE** *comes towards* **SAM** *pulls her hand jokey-lazy like "hurry up," shuffles out.* **SAM** *watches him start to exit with a smile.* **LEO** *looks away and respectfully lets them have a little private moment.)*

MIKE. *(As he disappears into Sam's room, kindly.)* 'Night, Leo.

LEO. *(Sincere.)* 'Night, man.

> (**SAM** *looks at her door. She is into* **MIKE**.*)*

I can't believe he's not circumcised!

SAM. Oh for god's sake. It actually feels really – / I'm never telling you anything again.

LEO. / I like him though.

SAM. Yeah, me too. He's kind of great. Like, he's a little dorky, but not a dork-dork.

LEO. Totally. And I like that he's funny, but he's not an upstager.

SAM. No! I know. And he doesn't care that he's fifth.

LEO. Fifth?

SAM. *(Counting on her fingers.)* My career, the novel, you and friends and stuff, the blog, making money, him. You know...sixth.

LEO. What about your family?

SAM. They're a close seventh. If it's the holidays, they move to third.

LEO. I don't know. I call bullshit. I think you're doing that thing again where you are pretending to be more women's lib than you are. You've read *The Twilight Saga* / three times and saw all the movies in the theater. You're not exactly Gloria Steinem.

SAM. Okay. I just like vampire mythology. I always have. Anne Rice.

Whatever. A boyfriend is certainly NOT all I need in life.

(Pause.)

But can I tell you one thing he said to me that's so cute I want to die and then we should totally talk about your writing again?

LEO. Of course. Tell me immediately.

SAM. Okay so the other day when we woke up, he had to get up early but I didn't. So he like got up and took a shower and stuff and he came back in and crawled into bed for a minute and I rolled over to like say hi and stuff. And he goes, "I have a secret for you." And I was like, "what" and then he goes, "you're pretty great."

LEO. That's revolting

SAM. And like. LEO. It was literally like…I had to actually summon every ounce of feminism inside me to not scream MARRY ME PLEASE in his face.

LEO. Totally.

SAM. Okay. I'm going to look away from you now because I can't believe I even told you that and I know I'm going to completely regret it because it's so sappy and weird and I want to pretend I never told you so let's talk about your writing instead and never mention this moment.

(She looks away for a moment, pausing. After a second.)

LEO. Do I respond to you...or?

SAM. No.

LEO. Okay.

(She takes a moment. Then. She is ready. She turns back to him. All business.)

SAM. Okay. WRITING. Let's make a deal. Every day for the next month, we will write together for ONE HOUR. I'll work on the novel and you'll work on your poems –

LEO. I'm more excited about / the short stories lately

SAM. / Short stories then...for ONE HOUR a day no matter what.

LEO. Yes. Thank you. THANK. YOU. This is good.

SAM. Totally. It just keeps the muscle going. And I could use more dedicated time, you know.

LEO. And I have ideas.

SAM. You always do.

*(**SAM** takes one more hit from the bowl and stands.)*

We should go to bed. It's late.

*(Possibility hangs in the air... **LEO** eyes her.)*

Fine. One more level.

LEO. Yesssssssss

*(**LEO** shifts on the couch to make room for her. She picks up the controller and plays. **LEO** watches. We hear the video game music.*)*

Sam. I will say this without looking at you. But.

I'm happy that Mike said that to you. You deserve someone who will say that to you.

*(**SAM** smiles to herself. After a second, **SAM** glances at **LEO**. He catches her. She looks away. He smiles to himself.)*

(Lights.)

---

* A license to produce *I Wanna Fucking Tear You Apart* does not include performance usage rights for any third-party or copyrighted video games. Licensees should create their own sound effects or use sound effects in the public domain.

April

(*This is a short scene. Like twenty seconds.*)

(**LEO** *and* **SAM** *play "It's Only Water."* **LEO**
*starts it as the lights come up. It gets intense.
They stand over the sink splashing like
idiots.*)

(*Then:*)

LEO. (*Affronted.*) HEY

HEY

STOP.

...We should get back to writing.

(*Lights.*)

---

* It's Only Water is a game where you splash water (from the sink, from a
glass, from wherever) and you yell "It's only water!" It is a childish game
my friends and I invented in college. The only rules are you have to yell
"It's only water!" every time you splash and you cannot use toilet water
and you cannot damage computers, tablets, or phones. "It's only water"
is short for "Why are you so mad, it's only water." You can feel free to
pepper that sentence in once to clarify the game.

May

(**LEO** *is sitting on the edge of the sink shirtless [perhaps]. He is watching* The Golden Girls *and clipping his toenails. He hums/sings something in the style of the theme song to himself.* The whole thing. Clip. Clip.)

(*The theme song ends.*)

(*Clip.*)

(*Lights.*)

---

* A license to produce *I Wanna Fucking Tear You Apart* does not include a performance license for any third-party or copyrighted recordings, music or images. Licensees must acquire rights for any copyrighted recordings or images or create their own.

June

(**SAM** *enters. She is sweaty. She looks like shit. Gross summer in New York shit.*)

SAM. *(Fumbling with keys in the door.)* Ugh I look like gross summer in New York shit and I need a fucking DRINK –

(**SAM** *looks up and sees* **CHLOE**, *cute, thin, blonde perhaps?, sitting cross-legged in front of the coffee table with a glass of white wine.*)

Oh, hello.

(I should take this opportunity to mention that **CHLOE** *is wearing shorts with leggings and it's like one hundred degrees out.)*

CHLOE. Hi! Oh! Hi! You must be Sam –

(**CHLOE** *scrambles to her feet and extends her hand.* **SAM** *shakes it.*)

SAM. Guilty. And you are –

CHLOE. Oh, I'm sorry! Haha! I've had two glasses so... I'm Chloe. Leo's –

SAM. Right...oh right, Leo's coworker.

CHLOE. *(A little joke.)* Guilty.

(**CHLOE** *sits back down and takes a sip of wine.*)

Leo just went to get some vodka. He'll be back in a minute.

We're making flirtinis.

SAM. Exotic.

(A tiny pause.)

CHLOE. Oh! But we have more wine still – do you want a glass?

SAM. No, I'm not much of a wine person.

(**SAM** *crosses to the fridge.*)

I will engage in a beer though. I will do that.

(**SAM** *grabs a beer.* **CHLOE** *shifts a little.*)

So you work with Leo.

CHLOE. Yup.

SAM. What a tool right?

CHLOE. *(Relieved* **SAM** *is making a joke.)* Totally.

SAM. Utter garbage.

CHLOE. Sometimes the sight of his face makes me physically ill.

SAM. Of course. Of course. That makes sense.

CHLOE. Well I mean he's ugly.

SAM. Disgusting.

CHLOE. So, like it's so hard to cope, you know? Around the office?

SAM. Oh, I do. I typically walk around here vomiting. And then just slip sliding around in it, hoping for a miracle.

(**LEO** *enters with flourish.*)

LEO. I HAVE OBTAINED MORE ALCOHOL CALM DOWN EVERYONE

DO NOT PANIC

CHLOE. My hero!

(**LEO** *sees* **SAM**.)

LEO. Sam! You're home! Did you meet Chloe?

SAM. No, we've been sitting here in silence waiting for you to / introduce us.

CHLOE. We're just girls. We don't know – we don't know what we're doing!

LEO. Har har, dickheads. Whatchu two talkin' about?

CHLOE.	**SAM**.
How hideous you are.	Vomit.

LEO. Aw, I'm touched.

> (**LEO** *puts away the alcohol.* **SAM** *goes to the couch and sits.* **CHLOE** *is still on the floor cross-legged with those damn leggings on. There's a bit of an awkward beat while* **SAM** *drinks her beer and they both sort of wait for* **LEO** *to join them. He comes over after he's made himself a drink. He sits.*)

My work wife and my home wife. In one room. I love it.

CHLOE. Your work wife? I'm honored.

LEO. You should be. I'm very selective, right Sam?

SAM. *(Taking a drink.)* You know it.

CHLOE. Glad I pass the test.

LEO. No one else hates that fuckface J.R. as much as you do. That's how I knew you were the one. The lucky gal I was going to work-marry. Sam, have I told you about J.R. – he's THE WORST.

SAM. No –

LEO. Well. He's one of those straight guys who's like "I'm a feminist."

CHLOE. And he is always like, quoting bell hooks and preaching about gender-inclusive bathrooms –

LEO. IT'S LIKE WE GET IT YOU ARE LIBERAL AND INFORMED AND SENSITIVE

CHLOE. But you know he totally goes home and like, jerks off to snuff porn.

(**LEO** *laughs and sort of play hits* **SAM**, *who coughs a little on the beer she's drinking.*)

LEO. See, told you, Chloe's the best.

CHLOE. Aw.

LEO. No seriously. I talk about you all the time. I'm like, a LITTLE obsessed with you.

CHLOE. *(To* **SAM**.*)* He talks about you constantly. To the point where I was like...nervous to meet you. / ahahaha

SAM. *Ahahaha*

Well, gee.

(*Small pause.* **SAM** *takes a drink.* **LEO** *gauges her and detects her mood for the first time. He attempts to salvage...*)

LEO. Sam. Chloe is the best writer in the department. / You guys have so much in common.

CHLOE. Oh, no – I'm the worst.

LEO. She's so funny. The top ten article she did last week. AH! Perfect! PER. FECT.

CHLOE. Ah, come on. I mean, we work at like shitty knockoff BuzzFeed it's not REAL. / We don't even use our real names on the bylines.

LEO. No. No! It was hilarious – "Top Ten Reasons White Guys Play Guitars While Wearing Shorts."

CHLOE. Oh, my college boyfriend, right? Ughhhh.

SAM. Pretty funny.

LEO. And oh my god – the PEN NAME YOU CHOSE FOR THAT ONE THE PEN NAAAAAME Tell her tell her tell herrrrr

CHLOE. Craig Santos.

> (**LEO** *erupts into laughter.*)

SAM. Is...should I know that / name or?

CHLOE. Sam, Leo tells me you're a writer too. A good writer.

LEO. *(To* **SAM**.*)* She's brilliant.

SAM. I mean, yeah, I'm basically the next Alice Munro, but just a lot less appealing / at parties –

LEO.	**CHLOE**.
(Genuine.) Hahah	Ah, no! Don't say that! No!

LEO. It's okay, Chloe, Sam loooooves to cast herself in the role of underdog. It keeps her young.

SAM. Or at least busy.

LEO. Haha.

LEO & CHLOE. Cheers!

SAM. Cheers.

> (*Slightly uncomfortable moment.* **CHLOE** *shifts around a little. They all take a sip.*)

LEO. Lime?

CHLOE. Yummy.

So Sam. What are you working on now?

LEO. She's working on her debut novel.

SAM. Right, if working means re-watching the Aidan seasons of *Sex and the City* over and over again.

CHLOE. OH MY GOD WHO ARE YOU /

SAM. I'm sorry what?

CHLOE. I BET YOU'RE A SAMANTHA! Everything Leo has told me about you suggests YOU. ARE. A. SAMANTHA.

But also! That's your ACTUAL NAME! So you must be!!

LEO. No, no. Sam is a Miranda. One hundred percent.

CHLOE. Wow. Wow.

She is the best one.

She is ABSOLUTELY the best one.

LEO. I know.

So you know I don't say that lightly.

CHLOE. I'm only a Charlotte.

SAM. You flatter me, Leo.

LEO. I only speak the truth.

CHLOE. So what's your novel about?

SAM. Well –

LEO. It's like – it has like a millennial *Bridget Jones' Diary* / feel. It's sort of hodge podgy. But also linear.

CHLOE. I love that movie!

SAM. It's sort of like a slice of this one girl's life. But it's through her text messages, emails, statuses and food / diaries.

CHLOE. I LOVE IT! OH GOD I LOVE IT! I LOVE THIS!

When can I read it?

SAM.	LEO.
Ohhh no… I don't –	Oh my god! Sam is super open, she'd love your feedback

CHLOE. Feedback. Anytime. I would love that. I would LOVE to give feedback. I would love to give feedback anytime!

SAM. That's…sweet.

LEO. Sam. Chloe is a genius. Like, you should totally have her read it, she's a great writer. She gives the best notes. And Chloe. Tell her.

CHLOE. Hm?

LEO. TELL HER ABOUT YOUR NOVEL!

CHLOE. Oh, jeez. Oh. Well, it's not cool like yours. It's just. Ah. And like, I've been stuck on it for years so –

LEO. Ah! Wait! Oh my god! Chlo-bird! Sam and I are doing this thing. This like, we give each other deadlines and stuff and like force each other to work. You should do it with us!

CHLOE. Oh my god. YES. I need that. I need that SO BADLY.

It's always difficult for me to motivate because the content is a *little* emotionally taxing for me.

SAM. Oh?

CHLOE. Ugh. I hate myself in advance for saying this, but, like, my novel is a sort of like…a collection of personal / anecdotes? Like, short um –

SAM. A…memoir?

CHLOE.	LEO.
No…	Chloe's had such a crazy life.

CHLOE. It's just. It's. I grew up in this really rich part of Maine? (I mean I wasn't rich. I wasn't.) But it was this like, super specific vacation-y place and my Mom was pretty demanding.

And. It's... I guess it's about that?

SAM. Sounds / great.

CHLOE. / AHHHHH I HATE MYSELF!!! Leo's been trying to get me to be better about putting myself out there. It's been such a challenge for me.

LEO. PREACH! PREACH! SING YOUR SONG FROM THE ROOFTOPS, GIRL!

CHLOE. *(Continuous.)* But he's a great cheerleader. / You're lucky you have him around ALL the time.

LEO. / Rah.

SAM. Mmmhmmm.

LEO. Oh Sam doesn't need me, she's like, the gross kind of person who has DISCIPLINE / or whatever.

SAM. Well, I don't know about THAT.

CHLOE. / UGH GOD REALLY?! I would DIE to be disciplined. Being disciplined is like, the number one thing I wish I WAS. How do you do it?

LEO. Well, Sam is freelance so she can write whenever she wants –

SAM. Well, that's not exactly true. / I have lots of work to do outside the novel so it's not like I have unlimited time.

LEO. Yeah, / but like, it kind of is.

CHLOE. Oooo! Freelance! Freelance what! I would love to be freelance! That's literally my dream.

SAM. I write copy. And grants. Some personal assisting work. But, I guess mostly I ghostwrite YA books. Like fantasy ones.

LEO. *Harry Potter Hunger Games* knockoffs.

SAM. Says the man who works at "BuzzFeed for dummies."

CHLOE. Haha! Oh my god. It totally is "BuzzFeed for dummies." TOTALLY. You're funny. God, you're so funny.

So wow. YA novels. That's cool.

SAM. Yeah but I hate most of what I write because it's watered-down trash for prepubescent fetuses.

LEO. Fetus-i?

SAM. You say potato, I say I may kill myself before my next deadline just to avoid using the phrase "featuring a scrappy young teen girl who holds the key to saving the universe" in an abstract one more time.

CHLOE. But still. Writing is writing. I've spent every second since I graduated trying to figure out how to do what you're doing. You're lucky! To get to sit with your thoughts and words every single day? What a gift!

LEO. And you're in your pajamas a lot, which I deeply envy.

CHLOE. Must save you big time on your clothing budget.

(There's a small pause.)

LEO. I love you guys hanging out. I love this.

CHLOE. Me too!

SAM. *(Taking a drink.)* ...

LEO. Ooo! Guess what! Sam has a hot boyfriend!

CHLOE. WHAT?! YOU DO! OH MY GOD! TELL ME ALL ABOUT HIM

SAM. Oh. I mean. Yeah, he's cool.

LEO. *(To **SAM**.)* He's HOT.

CHLOE. Ohmygod I'm so jealous. I want a hot boyfriend. I never date hot guys. You're so lucky. Ugh. You're so lucky.

LEO. He's in finance. FINANCE. Like. He's a real person.

(*Playfully to* **SAM**.) Even though he's not –

(**LEO** *makes a scissors gesture.*)

SAM.	**CHLOE**.
(*To* **LEO**, *under her breath.*) Now I get gay bashing.	(*Hitting* **SAM**.) Oh my god. I'm so jealous. I'm so jealous of you.

SAM. (*Reacting to Chloe's hit.*) Ow.

CHLOE. (*Not noticing Sam's "ow."*) I just. I only *sleep* with guys. I sleep with all these guys. Who just use me. Like, they're so mean to me. And I end up just feeling like shit about myself. I end up just being like "ugh why is it so hard" and being like "I'm gonna die alone." You're so lucky you have a hot nice boyfriend.

I would kill for that. I would. I mean it.

SAM. (*Getting a little icy.*) I don't think that's necessary. You seem perfectly capable of finding a boyfriend without bloodshed.

CHLOE. You'd think! You'd think!

SAM. I would.

(**CHLOE** *stands and crosses to* **SAM**, *slightly tipsy and invading her personal space.*)

CHLOE. No really though. How do you do it? HOW? What's your secret?

(**CHLOE** *drapes an arm around* **SAM** *who is clearly disgusted.*)

SAM. *(For shock value.)* I just fucking love to suck cock. I like to just take my tongue and trace it along the ridge. It's like a cotton candy stick of mag–

> **(LEO** *gets up and in between them, stopping her.* **SAM** *is smug.)*

LEO. Annnnnnd scene.

CHLOE. Blow jobs! The key to any man's heart!

> **(LEO** *leads* **CHLOE** *back to the couch. She sits on it.)*

I just. I don't like giving head that much. I just don't love it. / I wish I did. I wish I did.

SAM. *(Perhaps smugly to* **LEO**.*)* / Of course you don't.

CHLOE. *(Not hearing* **SAM**.*)* So that's it. That's how you got a hot boyfriend. That's how. Wow.

LEO. *(As a dig to* **SAM**.*)* Yup. When you've got a sort of Jafar personality, you've really gotta fine-tune / your oral skills.

CHLOE. *(To* **LEO**.*)* No! Leo! No!

Don't say that! No! She's not. She's not

…*fat.*

(To **SAM***, comforting.)* I didn't even. I didn't.

I didn't even notice that.

> *(Uhhhh.* **LEO** *never said she was fat. A bomb has just gone off.* **SAM** *looks at* **LEO***. Silence.)*

SAM. *(After a moment, looking directly at* **LEO**.*)* Hm. And here I was. Worried people could tell.

LEO. *(Silently begging her to not address it.)* Sam…

CHLOE. I mean, it's so great that he likes you for you. You know? I wish I could find a guy who likes me for me.

SAM. *(Rage coming through now a little.)* Actually, he likes me for the Ding Dongs and Ho Hos I keep under the / bed.

LEO. *(Rising.)* / Chloe, give me your phone, I'll order you an Uber.

CHLOE. *(Clocking the awkwardness, but not sure what happened.)*... Yeah, that's a good idea. I think I'm a little drunk. I'm such a lightweight.

SAM. So I've heard.

> *(**LEO** gives **SAM** a look like "knock it off.")*

CHLOE. I have to pee.

LEO. Oh, it's this way.

> *(**CHLOE** exits to the bathroom. There's a silence between **SAM** and **LEO**. He's about to say something. Then he doesn't. He looks at Chloe's phone instead, he goes over to get her purse.)*
>
> *(After a moment, **CHLOE** reenters from the bathroom.)*

Three minutes.

CHLOE. Oh, great. Thank you.

> *(She walks over to **SAM** and hugs her. Holds on to her.)*

It was so nice to meet you. I'm sorry I got drunk! I just. I never drink!

SAM. How sweet.

LEO. I have your purse.

CHLOE. You guys are. You guys are such fun friends. It's so nice.

(**CHLOE** *hugs* **LEO**.)

LEO. I'm gonna walk you down, okay?

CHLOE. You don't have to.

LEO. Of course I do, I'm a gentleman.

CHLOE. You are! You totally are!

(**CHLOE** *turns to* **SAM**.)

It was so nice meeting you. I'm sorry I got so drunk. I swear I never do that. I was just trying to keep up!

LEO. Alright, let's go before the cab pulls away, babe.

CHLOE. *(Turning back one last time.)* Okay. Bye Sam I can't wait to read your novel.

SAM. Sure.

CHLOE. *(Getting drunk-serious.)* No. Really. I can't wait.

(**CHLOE** *exits,* **LEO** *follows.* **LEO** *and* **SAM** *have a look – it's brief. Almost undetectable.* **SAM** *is alone. She walks over to the counter. Drinks her beer. Fidgets. Maybe cleans up a little. After a long moment alone.* **LEO** *returns.)*

SAM. *(Laughing.)* Really? Really?

LEO. What?

SAM. *(Imitating him and* **CHLOE**.*)* "Preach! Preach! Work!" "My mom was demanding."

LEO. I'm going to bed.

(**LEO** *gets his phone, crosses in front of* **SAM** *to go to his room.)*

SAM. *(Light.)* She is such a fucking idiot. Ha, I will actively kill you if you actually send her my novel.

LEO. *(Weary.)* Why does everything have to be so difficult with you?

SAM. *(Stunned he's not on her side.)* What?

LEO. Look I know she's. God, I just wanted to have someone over for a fucking drink. And you just. Why do you make it so hard to like, integrate you?

SAM. Why do *I* make it / hard?

LEO. / You could just let things go once in a while. You could, you know. You don't HAVE to fucking challenge EVERYTHING.

SAM. Leo –

      (He's gone.)

(Sort of stunned.) Fuck you.

      (She swigs her beer.)

      (Lights.)

July

(It's the dead of night. The living room is dark. A light through the window. Silence. From off, we hear clomping feet. Keys jangling. The door to the apartment swings open. It's **LEO**. *He stumbles in. He flicks on the light. He is wasted.)*

(He goes over to the fridge. His ass sticks out and he rummages for something. He eats something gross or drinks directly out of a carton or something drunk. He walks back into the living room. He jams his iPod into the speaker.)

(A song plays loudly.*)

SAM. *(From off.)* WHAT THE FUCK

(He keeps dancing.)

(From off.) I'M GOING TO ASSASSINATE YOU

(He turns it up. He dances offstage towards Sam's room. We hear a bounch of yelling, maybe some hitting as the song continues to play. He stumbles back into the living room after a second. She's clearly booted him out.

---

* In early workshops, "Bang Bang" by Jessie J, Ariana Grande and Nicki Minaj was used. In the Studio Theater production, a Skrillex Remix of Lady Gaga's "Bad Romance" was used, and in the Rivendell (Chicago) production they used "Joyful, Joyful" from *Sister Act 2*, but cut it down for time. It should be something both actors love that's very uptempo and from when they would have been in college. A license to produce *I Wanna Fucking Tear You Apart* does not include a performance license for any third-party or copyrighted music. Licensees should create an original composition or use music in the public domain. For further information, please see the Music and Third-Party Materials Use Note on page iii.

He goes back to the fridge, opens it and just stands there staring at it. Just then. **SAM** *enters wrapped in an afghan. She looks pissed. She stands there glaring at him. He looks back. The song is at full volume.)*

(Suddenly. A rap break or chorus or shift in the song starts. **SAM** *drops the afghan and begins to perfectly rap / dance it at* **LEO**. *She sort of rap-dance chases him around the room. He's delighted slash terrified. When the chorus drops back in they both join in sync, doing choreography. They finish with gusto. They both pant for a second.)*

SAM. I'm going to bed.

LEO. 'Night.

(They exit to their rooms.)

(Lights.)

August

> (**LEO** *sits on the floor, index cards and pages all around him.*)

LEO. *(Calling off to* **SAM**.*)* I think the Andrew chapter should go before the visit home status updates.

SAM. *(From off.)* I guess, but then it's sad thing then happy thing. Don't you think – just like – texture-wise, we want the reverse? Happy happy then BAM sad?

LEO. I guess. But that seems expected.

SAM. *(From off.)* Right but, I mean dare to be obvious.

LEO. True.

> (**SAM** *reenters.*)

How about – Andrew chapter, grocery list, THEN visit home status updates.

SAM. Wow.

Okay.

Wow.

So. Wait?

Then what goes in the second chapter instead of grocery list?

LEO. Nothing.

SAM. What?

LEO. It just goes drunk realization, harboring a fugitive –

SAM & LEO. Moment alone with the important ex!

SAM. I mean.

LEO. *(Tentatively surveying the cards.)* I mean.

I think it maybe works?

(**SAM** *lies on the ground and groans.*)

SAM. AHHHHHHHHHHHH FINALLY

CAN THIS BE REAL

CAN I BE ALMOST DONE

LEO. I feel like if you finish up those final edits –

SAM. I actually MIGHT be ready to submit 'er.

LEO. Fuck. It's about time.

SAM. Three years in the making.

(*A small pause as they look at the notecards.*)

LEO. I'm so proud of you, Sam. This is pretty amazing.

SAM. Maybe now I'm an inch closer to ditching all these awful day jobs.

LEO. Get that book advance, girl!

SAM. You hear about Lola?

LEO. The twelve-year-old sexy fictional character?

SAM. That's Lolita dumbass. LOLA sold her novel and got ONE HUNDRED FIFTY THOUSAND BUCKS. I wouldn't have to write any shitty *Divergent* things for like five years. I could even unblock all the Sallie Mae collection numbers from my phone. And I could just write. Like, I could just actually be a real writer. Who even KNOWS what I could do with all that time –

LEO. That's a lot of Mario.

SAM. I've had a job since I was twelve. I literally can't even imagine what my life would look like – how much more creative I'd be. It's actually, like, the dream.

LEO. (*Genuine.*) And here you are, ten steps closer.

SAM. I could NOT have done it without you. You're the best editor in the universe. Partner. In. Crime.

LEO. Aw, shucks.

> (**SAM** *gets up to pour herself a cup of coffee.*)

SAM. You want?

LEO. No. Jesus. I have the shakes. I can't believe you're having more.

SAM. I mean, I can't feel my eyeballs, but I feel like I could watch *Avatar* and not fall asleep –

LEO. Kinky.

SAM. I never had a thing for furries, but those little blue tails. UNGHHH.

> (*She sits back down with him.*)

LEO. Enough. Let's get serious.

You wanna quit these jobs and change your life, HUNNY so we gotta set deadlines.

It's important to have goals.

YOU always say it's important to have goals.

Let's talk about the deadline for your edits and the deadline for me to give you the "Tuesday Night at Nowhere Bar" story. I'm thinking two weeks.

> (*He flips open his planner. She opens up her iPhone calendar.*)

SAM. Great, but it's gonna take me some time / to give you notes on that. I have lots of deadlines coming up and...so.

LEO. / Oh come on. Surely you can –

> (*He registers her comment.*)

Right.

> (*A silence.*)

SAM. I'm not trying to be a cunt, Leo.

LEO. You're not.

SAM. I...

Do you want me to not talk about it?

LEO. What? No. I'm happy for you.

SAM. I know. I know you are.

You've been great.

It's. It's just. I know it would be hard for me. If it were, like, reversed.

LEO. I mean, sure I wish I was having the

You know *Traction* you're having. Right now.

I wish I was.

But this is great. You're my best friend. You're my sister.

We're on the same team.

Team. YOU.

And you're having this moment. And I'm seriously, genuinely happy for you.

(He means this. He is happy for her.)

SAM. Also it's dumb. Getting a legit fiction agent? It's not like a REAL THING. It literally means nothing. I basically just feel like I got a personal assistant. Which is nice. But hardly career-making.

LEO. Ha.

(There's a pause.)

SAM. It's gonna happen for you.

LEO. Ha, yeah.

SAM. I'm serious. / You're too good for it not to. The cream rises to the top.

LEO. Sam. It's me. I don't need that.

SAM. Seriously. Who do you know over forty or forty-five / that's like, toiling away in obscurity who is actually talented?

LEO. That's simplistic. Morgan Freeman did his first film at fifty.

SAM. Yeah, but like a writer?

LEO. Derek Myer.

SAM. No, I mean WE hate him. But he just like, had that big Indie Book Award and stuff.

LEO. True. I guess it depends how you define "obscurity."

(He thinks.)

Finland DeMurier.

SAM. Dude, she's our age.

LEO. WHAT?! WOW. Then what's with all the pastels?

SAM. I am unclear.

LEO. I didn't know.

SAM. For real, Leo. You're gonna be okay.

LEO. I'm actually okay now.

(A silence.)

Sorry. So. When do you think you can get me your notes?

SAM. You know what – never mind my deadlines. I will bump you to the top of the list.

LEO. Thanks.

(With a pause and a pretty please face.)

Just make sure you also leave time to clean my room?

SAM. *(Smiling.)* LEO! Again? I just did it last week!

LEO. I know I knooooow. Manic searching for my tight long-sleeved red t-shirt that looks effortless but isn't DESTROYED all your hard work.

SAM. It's in the tub on top of your wardrobe labeled "sweaters."

LEO. Abusive.

SAM. *(Anticipating his qualm.)* Long-sleeved is almost a sweater.

LEO. Hm. Interesting concept.

> (**LEO** *gets up with his coffee cup. He puts it in the sink. He pauses and doubles back to* **SAM**. *She is texting on her phone. He gives her a giant hug from behind. She places her arms on his.)*

(Softening, sincere.) I do love you. I love you so.

SAM. I love you too.

> *(Lights.)*

September

(**SAM** *sits on the couch with her phone. She texts. For a long while. Glances at the door. Sets the phone on the table. Turns on the TV. Watches* The Great British Bake Off *for a minute.* Picks up the phone again. Texts. Mutes Bake Off. For some reason. It is easier to text when the TV is on mute. I don't know why. But let's admit it.)

(*It is easier to text when the TV is on mute.*)

(**SAM** *sets the phone down. Unmutes it. Watches for thirty seconds. Restless, she shuts off the TV. Checks her phone one more time. Just then...*)

(**LEO** *enters. He sees her. He goes to plug his phone into the charger.*)

SAM. Where have you been?

LEO. My phone died, sorry.

SAM. We had plans.

LEO. *My phone died.*

SAM. We were supposed to write together.

LEO. You could have started without me.

SAM. Duh, I know. But that's not what *writing together* means.

(*She pauses, realizes.*)

---

* A license to produce *I Wanna Fucking Tear You Apart* does not include a performance license for any third-party or copyrighted recordings or images. Licensees must acquire rights for any copyrighted recordings or images or create their own.

SAM. Were you with him again?

Leo. I thought after last time you swore you'd never see him again. He's toxic. No sex is worth this, Leo.

LEO. No. God. I wasn't with Josh.

I got drinks with some work people.

SAM. Work people?

LEO. Work. People.

SAM. Your best pal Chloe.

LEO. And Ben. And Stephanie. And Teresa – MY BOSS.

I had to go.

SAM. Had to?

LEO. I mean not like, concentration camp had to. But professionally had to.

SAM. You don't even like your job.

> (**LEO** *doesn't respond. He starts to make himself a sandwich.*)

Lately you've been avoiding me. I don't like it.

LEO. You're being paranoid.

SAM. Don't gaslight me.

LEO. We're not like *in a relationship* I don't CONSTANTLY have to tell you where I am and who I'm with.

SAM. I know that. Don't make me feel pathetic.

LEO. You said it not me.

SAM. Why are you being so mean?

LEO. It's called a joke.

SAM. We made plans and you stood me up. That's rude.

> (**LEO** *rolls his eyes.*)

LEO. You're right. You're always right. I'm gonna go to bed.

>   (**LEO** *walks off to his room. He's gone.* **SAM** *eats another Pringle.*)
>
>   (*He renters suddenly.*)

It pisses me off you think I'm jealous of you.

I'm not.

I'm not jealous of you or your agent.

SAM. It pisses me *off you* think I'm jealous of *you.*

I'm not.

Of your friends. Or your happy hours.

LEO. Now you're going to think I AM jealous of you. Because I brought it up.

SAM. You're going to think I'm jealous of you, too. Because I brought it up back.

LEO. So what do we do?

>   (*Lights.*)

October

(Lights up on **SAM** *and* **LEO** *mid-fight.* **SAM** *is dressed as a giant box of popcorn. She has popcorn glued all over her shoulders. She is wearing a refrigerator box.* **LEO** *is dressed as a doctor. He has a nametag that reads "McDreamy.")*

LEO. WELL HAPPY FUCKING HALLOWEEN

SAM. YOU CAN SAY THAT AGAIN

LEO. HAPPY FUCKING HALLOWEEN

SAM. FUCK YOU.

LEO.   I DIDN'T KNOW WE HAD OFFICIALLY DECIDED

SAM. OH PLEASE YOU KNEW YOU FUCKING KNEW

LAST YEAR WAS HORSE AND JOCKEY THE YEAR BEFORE THAT WAS MULDER AND SCULLY AND THE YEAR BEFORE THAT WAS A PAIR OF SNEAKERS.

EVERY. YEAR.

WE DO THIS EVERY YEAR

THIS WAS AN AGGRESSIVE CHOICE ON YOUR PART, LEO

LEO. WHY DO YOU ALWAYS ASSUME I'M OUT TO GET YOU

SAM. WHY DO YOU ALWAYS MINIMIZE IT WHEN I'M UPSET WITH YOU

LEO. IT'S A FUCKING PARTY. IT'S SUPPOSED TO BE FUN IT'S NOT A BIG DEAL

SAM. NOT TO YOU! YOU'RE NOT THE ONE WHO SHOWED UP DRESSED LIKE A GIANT FUCKING BOX OF JIFFY POP

LEO. WELL EVEN IF I HAD DONE WHAT WE'D SUPPOSEDLY PLANNED, YOU WOULD STILL LOOK RIDICULOUS

SAM. YES, BUT IT WOULD HAVE MADE SENSE IT WOULD HAVE MADE SENSE

LEO. HOW SO? HOW THE FUCK SO?!

SAM. POPCORN AND SODA. POPCORNANDSODA. IT GOES TOGETHER. I CAN'T FUCKING – ARGHHHHH – I CAN'T BELIEVE YOU ARE GOING TO PRETEND YOU DON'T KNOW THIS IS A HUGE STAB IN THE BACK.

LEO. YOU ARE SO DRAMATIC. MAKING ME CHASE YOU OUT OF A PARTY IN FRONT OF –

SAM. YOU FUCKING WENT AS PATRICK DEMPSEY. TO HER FUCKING MEREDITH GREY.

NOTHING.

AND I MEAN.

NOTHING.

IS SACRED TO YOU.

CLEARLY.

LEO. *(Flipping out.)* OH MY GOD. YOU'RE SUCH A CHILD. I FORGOT. I FUCKING FORGOT. I FORGOT ABOUT POPCORN AND SODA. I FUCKING FORGOT OKAY?!!? OKAY!!!!! I FUCKINGGGGGG FORGOOOOOTTTTTTT

> *(Her phone beeps. The fight pauses. She goes to it. She texts.)*

Mike?

SAM. Yes.

> *(She keeps texting. She glares up at him. Goes back to texting. He sits on the couch.)*

LEO. I'm sorry I went to the party with her. I did it on purpose.

SAM. I know you did.

LEO. I guess I wanted to see if you still loved me.

SAM. I do.

LEO. It makes me feel happy you were jealous of her.

SAM. That's evil of you.

LEO. I know.

SAM. Stop using her against me. You have to stop. You do it all the time. I fucking HATE her. SHE WILL RUIN US. SHE IS THE NEXT YOKO ONO. / I FEEL IT IN MY BONES.

LEO. / You're so full of hyperbole. I've been friends with you for almost fifteen years now and I swear, I've never heard you say a single in-proportion thing the entire time.

SAM. Leo. It's scaring me how much you don't seem to understand why she.

AHHHHHHHHH

LEO. She what? *(Sighing.)* Come on, Sam.

All mind games aside.

She's our kind of people. I swear. She's one of us.

> *(Pause.)*

I'm seriously not saying that to be a dick. I'm just saying, she's actually pretty great. I genuinely think that you could like her. And this is ME telling you that.

(**SAM** *snorts.*)

LEO. What?

SAM. Leo. Leo she's.

LEO. She's what?

SAM. She's someone we used to make fun of. Like in college. We would have crucified her.

LEO. She's nice. And talented.

(*He pauses fractionally.*)

And supportive.

SAM. Are you saying I'm not supportive?

LEO. No.

I'm not saying that.

You are. It's just.

I never believe it. I never believe the support from you.

It's comes through...complicated-ly.

(*She looks upset.*)

SAM. Okay. I guess I wish I knew what that meant.

LEO. Don't do that... Don't make that upset face. Jesus. This is why I can never.

This is why.

I can't talk to you about this stuff. You get upset.

SAM. Well, yeah, I mean. The person.

My person.

The person who means the most in the universe to me.

Thinks when I'm SINCERELY being supportive, I'm secretly undermining him.

LEO. Wow, I don't remember saying that.

SAM. This is your gay man trauma speaking.

I feel this is your gay man trauma speaking.

I love you so much. I wish you knew.

I wish you could believe that I love you unconditionally.

LEO. *(Really honest here, not punishing.)* I'm not sure we have the same definition of unconditionally.

SAM. Wow.

> *(Pause.)*

Listen. I know I'm judgmental. I'm the most judgmental person on the planet.

But that stops at your feet.

I draw the fucking line right there at your toes. I swear.

I fucking SWEAR, Leo.

> *(And here? There's a shift. A façade that melts away for this moment.)*

The only true thing. The only real thing I have is you, Leo. I mean that.

Agents. Books. Boys.

I don't care. I fucking don't care.

I would give up everything for you.

All of it.

You're the only real thing.

You are the only thing that is real to me.

> *(He shifts, uncertain.)*

Leo.

SAM. You're the only person who gets that people.

People like her.

They walk through the world as winners.

They get awards and weddings and smiles and designer things and waves and free drinks at bars and nannying jobs and huge adorable sweaters and babies and when they walk into a room they are *wanted*.

But us? The gay kid? The fat girl?

That's not our story.

But when you're with me.

When you're on my team –

LEO. Team fat/gay –

SAM. *(Smiles.)* Yes.

Our team makes me feel like I can do it. I can battle my way through.

I can stay up later.

I can work harder.

I can be as fucking incredible as I need to be to catch up

With those Elizabeths and Kimberlys and Annas... those Chloes

(She pauses for second.)

But without you –

I don't know if I can. I don't know if there's a point.

(Long silence.)

LEO. I don't want to break up with you.

SAM. Then don't. Please. I'm begging you.

(Lights.)

November

*(**SAM** enters. She's carrying a bunch of groceries that obscure her vision of the room. She struggles. **CHLOE** is sitting on the couch. She rushes up to help.)*

SAM. LEO LEO OPEN Help me I missed the delivery cutoff time and they made me carry them myself. THIS IS THE LAST TIME I GO TO THE KEY FOODS INSTEAD OF A REAL GROCERY STORE –

*(She notices it's **CHLOE** helping, not **LEO**. Throughout the scene, **SAM** is trying to be nice.)*

CHLOE. Let me help you.

SAM. Chloe...hi.

CHLOE. Hey! Whoa – lotta groceries there.

SAM. Writing weekend. Stocking up.

(The girls walk with the groceries to the kitchen.)

CHLOE. Pumpkin spice K-cups? Who knew?

SAM. Right?

So.

CHLOE. Oh sorry. I'm not being creepy. Leo went to buy cigarettes.

SAM. Cigarettes? Really?

CHLOE. I think?

Maybe I'm wrong.

SAM. No. No. You're probably right.

*(Pause. A little awkward. **SAM** tries her best...)*

SAM. How's work. And everything?

CHLOE. It's good. I mean, you know. Thank God for Leo. THANK GOD. He's what gets me through the day.

SAM. He's the best.

CHLOE. He is.

I mean. Except for the fact that he hums aloud ALL DAY and doesn't realize it.

SAM. Haha, yeah he does do that.

CHLOE. And he eats smelly tuna sandwiches.

SAM. But. He puts potato chips in them. So. You have to give him some points there.

CHLOE. Haha true.

> *(Another little lull.* **SAM** *starts putting the groceries away.)*

You need help?

SAM. I got it. There's not too many.

CHLOE. Cool.

> *(Lull again.* **SAM** *cracks a Diet Coke.)*

Oh! God! I forgot to say.

I read the novel!

Your novel, I mean.

Leo sent it to me.

I hope that's okay.

SAM. He told me.

CHLOE. It was great. Like, really great.

SAM. Thank you.

CHLOE. You have such a voice. I mean it.

SAM. Wow, thanks.

CHLOE. You're so funny. I could never be funny like that. Asparagus fricassee?

SAM. Leo says you're very funny.

CHLOE. Ha. Maybe. But no.

Your novel.

It's so good. I wish I could write like you.

I could write and write and write for YEARS and it would never be so brave, you know?

SAM. I do.

CHLOE. And also the language – it's paradigm shifting.

I don't know if Leo told you but, um. A good friend of mine.

From Vassar.

He's in publishing. At Random House.

I could send it.

I could send it to him if you wanted.

SAM. Thanks, that's nice of you.

CHLOE. I mean, Leo's a good friend now so. And it's good. It's really good. So it would be my pleasure.

SAM. That's sweet. Thanks. I'll let you know.

CHLOE. Oh! How's your hot boyfriend? Mike, right?

SAM. He's good.

He'd be happy to know he's immortalized as "my hot boyfriend."

(**SAM** *sips her Diet Coke.*)

CHLOE. Of course.

It's cool that you guys are moving in together. That's pretty serious.

SAM. *(Choking a little on the Coke.)* What?

Oh. No.

We're not um. We're not doing that.

CHLOE. Oh? No. Oh. I'm sorry. Shit. I thought.

SAM. Did Leo say that?

CHLOE. Well...I thought he did? When he was asking about moving into my apartment. I thought he said the reason was because your boyfriend was moving in.

SAM. The reason for what? What?

CHLOE. The reason Leo's looking for a pla–

> *(She stops mid-sentence. She realizes in the moment that this is news to* **SAM**.*)*

Oh, you know. I think I was thinking of another coworker.

There's this cute guy in marketing. He's got a beard, too.

> *(A miniscule beat.)*

SAM. No, no. You're. You heard it right. Leo is looking for a place. I'm just.

> *(A pause.)*

I'm going to try living alone.

I need the extra room for a space. Like an office space.

Need some quiet to write, you know?

Without roommates. Distractions.

CHLOE. *(Visibly relieved.)* Ohhhhh yeah totally

That makes total sense

I get distracted too.

All the time.

By my roommate.

> (**SAM** *turns back to the groceries. Trying to pull herself together a little. There's a silence.* **LEO** *enters back in.*)

LEO. BRRRR It's colder than a witch's tit in a brass bra.

> (*He goes over to the sink to wash his hands, stepping by* **SAM**, *he playfully hip checks her.*)

What's the good word, friends?

CHLOE. We were just chatting about Sam's AMAZING novel!

LEO. *(Re:* **SAM** *for being so talented.)* What a cunt, right?

CHLOE.	**SAM**.
Yikes! The c word –	*(Trying to pull it together.)* Cunt? I'm honored.

LEO. Chlo.

Would you hate me if I changed before we head out?

CHLOE. Well, you look great, but the start time is loose. It's better to be a little late anyway.

LEO. Good. I'll be fast.

> (**LEO** *starts off to the bathroom.* **CHLOE** *hops up on the counter and sits.*)

CHLOE. No rush. Take your time.

LEO. *(Moving in slow motion.)* I always do.

CHLOE. Oh my god. You're such an idiot.

LEO. I'm not an idiot. I just look like one.

> (**LEO** *attempts a balletic kick.*)

CHLOE. Oh, sickled foot.

LEO. How dare you.

> *(The two girls sit in silence for a second. They look expectantly at one another. The both speak at the same time:)*

CHLOE.	**SAM**.
So where are you from again?	Would you mind if I went to my room?
Oh, god, no of course.	Rhode Island.
Oh, the tiny state!	Yeah, I just. I have some writing to do.

> *(Pause. **CHLOE** giggles, a little embarrassed.)*

CHLOE. Yeah, go ahead. I can entertain myself. When the muses call...

SAM. Ha, yeah. You gotta write when you can, right?

CHLOE. Right!

Write!

> *(**SAM** doesn't really get the joke. Since it only makes sense written.)*

SAM. What?

CHLOE. Nothing, ha, nevermind.

> *(**SAM** starts to exit to her room. **CHLOE** stops her, hopping off the counter.)*

Hey. Wait. One second? Before you go?

SAM. What's up?

CHLOE. Um. I'm sorry. I just. I have to ask.

I have to ask because it's been driving me nuts.

SAM. Okay...

CHLOE. Why. Um.

Why do you hate me?

> (*A deadly silence.*)

It's just.

Most people like me.

I'm actually nice. I know people say they're nice when really they're mean girls.

I'm not a mean girl. I wasn't even a mean girl in high school.

I was just quiet.

So. Yeah.

People generally like me.

And it's been making me MENTAL...

Like I've been BEATING my BRAINS out. To try to get you to like me.

I know I shouldn't care that you don't. But.

I care what people think of me.

But I guess I just want to know why.

Why you don't like me?

> (**SAM** *is quiet.*)

(*A joke to try and lighten.*) "Chloe, I don't hate you!"

> (*Another bit of silence.*)

SAM. I don't know what to say to that.

CHLOE. Okay. Wow.

SAM. I think this conversation is a bad idea.

SAM. I'm going to go write.

Have fun, okay?

> (**SAM** *starts to go.*)

CHLOE. Wait. Stop. I'm sorry.

Please. You can be honest.

I'm one of those people when I say, "You can be honest", I really mean it.

> (*Silence. We hear as* **LEO** *sings from the shower.*[*] **SAM** *takes a breath.*)

SAM. Okay.

You want me to be honest?

I really, sincerely don't hate you.

I just.

I don't give two fucks about you.

You see, girls like you. You're all the same.

You confuse DISINTEREST for DISLIKE.

I AM DISINTERESTED IN YOU.

I know. I know this must come as a great shock.

You walk around with people wanting to know more about you

SAM. With people asking about you

And caring about you

And people *generally liking you*

---

[*] A license to produce *I Wanna Fucking Tear You Apart* does not include a performance license for any third-party or copyrighted music. Licensees should create an original composition or use music in the public domain. For further information, please see the Music and Third-Party Materials Use Note on page iii.

As you say.

But I am not one of those people.

Because I know you.

I know your kind and I'm not impressed.

You are not *impressive* to me.

Because you and I.

We are not the same.

We're not some sort of "fun sisters in the fight."

I am not *generally liked.*

And I do not *generally like you.*

And that's OKAY.

Not everyone has to like you.

Maybe you need to think a little less about being liked, and a little more about being a fucking

INTERESTING human.

> *(**LEO** enters back in from changing in his room.)*

LEO. Chlo, I went back and forth. I know we're both wearing plum.* Are we too matchy-matchy?

> *(He looks at **CHLOE**. He can tell something went horribly wrong.)*

Everything okay here?

CHLOE. *(Trying to mask it.)* Of course. You?

You ready to go?

---

* Change to the color of the costume designer's preference! ☺

LEO. Yeah. You sure you're good?

CHLOE. Yeah. Let's blow this popsicle stand.

> *(**CHLOE** goes to get her bag. **LEO** eyes **SAM** like, "what the fuck happened?" **SAM** shrugs. **LEO** crosses to the door and opens it. **CHLOE** walks out. She pauses at the door frame, turns to **SAM**.)*

Have a nice night, Sam.

> *(**CHLOE** hurriedly walks out. **LEO** lingers, makes sure she's out the door.)*

LEO. What did you say?

> *(**SAM** doesn't answer. **LEO** sighs, frustrated and shakes his head.)*

Whatever.

> *(**LEO** starts to close the door to go.)*

SAM. Were you going to tell me you were moving out?

> *(He stops.)*

Were you?

LEO. Let's talk about this later.

SAM. No. I want to talk about it now. I've put fucking fifteen years into this friendship. That's a lot of real estate. That's a big fucking investment, and I deserve / an answer from you.

LEO. / Oh my god – here we fucking go, Sam the martyr.

SAM. NO.

NO.

NO.

NO.

I won't let you reduce this. I won't let you act like this is nothing to you and I'm overreacting.

LEO. I'm NOT acting like this OR you is nothing to me, Sam. What if I actually think it would be better for us if we had some space? We're not in our college dorm room. Sometimes it's nice to feel like an individual, you know. Sometimes I'd like to not feel like some weird conjoined twin with you. Like, this isn't normal! WHERE THE FUCK IS YOUR FUCKING BOYFRIEND ANYWAY? WHY DON'T YOU GO FUCK HIM? BLOW OFF SOME FUCKING STEAM! GET A FUCKING LIFE THAT ISN'T ME!

SAM. You know exactly what you're doing Leo. You are choosing that regular girl over me.

PLEASE do me a favor and just admit it.

PLEASE.

LEO. I'm not choosing. I can have more than one friend. We're not like, exclusive.

I can have different friends for different days.

SAM. *(Desperate to articulate.)* No but you can't though.

Because that's the point – we are exclusive

We get to be on our island where we are smarter and better than everyone.

And that's better than being thin.

Or straight.

Or normal, or whatever.

Because when we have each other IT DOESN'T MATTER THAT WE'RE BOTH FUCKING FREAKS.

> (**SAM** *pauses, she realizes she is a little scary.*)

SAM. *(Quietly.)* I mean. I know that's. But you know what I mean.

>   *(Silence. After a bit...)*

LEO. *(Treading lightly.)* I've actually never thought of it like that.

>   (**SAM** *looks at him. Hard.)*

SAM. You're so lucky. You get to walk through the world as like a sexy fun gay man –

LEO. Uh, whoa, okay?

SAM. Just. You're gorgeous. And you can pass for normal.

LEO. If you think I walk around a gay man dripping in normal person privilege, I don't even know what to say –

SAM. You know what I mean! You pass! People want you at parties. There's bars named after your cock / and stuff –

LEO. After MY cock?

SAM. You have a community. You get... There's no such thing as a fat bar.

LEO. *(Not mean.)* I don't know, I've been to KFC.

SAM. *(All one thought with her thought above.)* I'm trying to say... I don't know what I'm trying to say.

UGH. God, I fucking hate needing you this much. I hate it. There are so many terrible things happening in the world and I'm obsessing over this. Over you.

I should go make a fucking donation to the ACLU or something.

>   *(Another long silence.)*

LEO. *(Genuinely torn.)* I'm...I'm moving out. January first.

I didn't want to tell you like this.

I'm sorry.

>   *(Silence.)*

Sam, say something.

>   *(Silence.)*

She's. She's waiting downstairs.

SAM. Go.

>   *(He leaves. She watches him go. Maybe there's
>   a breath here. This is the first time she feels
>   absolutely alone.)*
>
>   *(Lights.)*

December

(**LEO** *is alone. He's antsy. Anxious. Perhaps he paces. Then settles for a moment just as* **SAM** *unlocks the door to the apartment.*)

SAM. *(As she puts her bag down.)* Hey stranger.

LEO. Hey.

SAM. I feel like I haven't seen you in weeks. What's new?

LEO. *(Gathering some stuff to head to his room.)* Same old, same old.

In the mail pile there's a delivery slip for you.

Some floral place.

SAM. *(Going over/looking at it.)* Oh.

LEO. From Mike?

SAM. My mom.

LEO. Linda, ay? What's the occasion?

SAM. Oh. I.

I'm sorry I didn't tell you.

I sold the book.

LEO. *(Stops exiting.)* What? Wow. Sam. That's so great. That's fucking great!

SAM. I'm excited.

LEO. How much you gettin'?!

SAM. TBD. Debut novel by a nobody? I'm hoping to get a happy meal out of it.

LEO. Now, now. At least go for a value meal. Know your worth.

SAM. Ha. True.

(*Fractal pause.*)

SAM. Wanna watch something?

LEO. No. I, uh. I should write.

> (**LEO** *heads towards his room,* **SAM** *gently stands in front of him, blocking him.*)

SAM. Everything okay?

LEO. Sure. Yes.

SAM. Doesn't seem like it.

LEO. (*Trying to pass.*) I don't want to rain on your parade.

SAM. (*Moving to block him again.*) I hate parades.

LEO. It's stupid.

SAM. (*Not moving to let him pass.*) ...

LEO. (*Irritated, he gives in.*) Fine. It's Chloe.

Like a couple weeks ago she basically stopped speaking to me at work.

And then today when I got to work her desk was empty. And fuckwad J.R. told me she quit. She apparently gave her two weeks notice...two weeks ago, I guess. Obviously. I can't believe she didn't even tell me. I thought we were fucking FRIENDS.

...I think she blocked me on Facebook.

SAM. Maybe she just left it.

LEO. She would never.

> (*A pause. Then...*)

I just...did something happen that night she came over Sam?

She was acting super weird after that. And like, I *know* you. I know you're – Harsh.

SAM. Like what could I have even said that would make her like stop talking to you and quit her job?

LEO. I don't know. *(Makes a sigh/thinking sound.)*

SAM. Maybe you made a joke or something that offended her. You can sometimes cross the line and not know it.

LEO. I'm not sure. I can't. I can't remember anything like that.

       (A small pause.)

SAM. Maybe she quit because she fucking hated working at some pointless dead-end fucking piece of shit time-wasting internet content monster. Maybe she found something better to do.

LEO. You really have a particular way of making me feel like shit / sometimes. It's almost impressive –

SAM. Okay fine I'm sorry. It was a joke, geez. Leo, relax.

It's probably not you, it's her. Don't let it eat you alive.

Just let her go.

At the end of the day, who is she?

LEO. I mean, she was my friend.

SAM. Yeah, but Leo. I mean, come on. What happens when she turns thirty and freaks out and marries the homophobic frat guy and you get sent off on the proverbial gay iceberg to fucking Fire Island or whatever?

LEO. *(Reluctantly snickering.)* It would be a beautiful wedding. I bet she'd let me be an usher.

SAM. That dumb bitch would probably have red velvet cake.

LEO. Ew no. It would be a fucking cupcake tower.

SAM. *(Laughs.)* Uh. The worst. I want a whole cake, like a piece of actual cake.

LEO. Mm. Of course.

> *(Small pause. **LEO** shifts. Bites his nail.)*

SAM. You want me to clean your room? It's been awhile. I'm itching for a little OCD therapy.

LEO. No. That's kind of...a lot right now.

SAM. We could go to a movie? I'll pay?

LEO. I'm not really in the mood.

SAM. Or drinks! / We could get some drinks.

LEO. SAM just. Jesus. KNOCK IT OFF. I'm fine. Stop like, pitying / me.

SAM. I'm not pitying –

LEO. You and I. We don't like, "get / drinks."

SAM. Why not? I'm a person, we're people, we could get drinks, I'd get / a drink with you.

LEO. No. Just. No.

I.

You're not exactly a resource for this problem.

I know you hated her.

I know you're secretly glad –

SAM. I'm not glad.

I'm not GLAD you're upset.

Leo!

Come on. Look, it's ME.

I'm not your enemy, I never have been.

You're moving out.

SAM. Can't your last few weeks be...

Can't we just be normal? Please?

> *(A silence. Perhaps **LEO** starts to cry. Or hit himself on the head. Or rock back and forth. Something a little disturbing.)*

(Worried.) Leo, what's wrong!?

LEO. I don't.

I don't even know where to begin.

SAM. Try.

LEO. I mean.

I guess...

I'm sure it's obvious that...I was moving in with Chloe.

SAM. Yeah, I mean, I figured.

LEO. I gave her a deposit and everything.

But now...

Now.

SAM. "Now" what?

LEO. It was everything I had! And now she's gone!

SAM. Are you fucking kidding me? How much was it?!

LEO. First and last months, plus a deposit.

> *(Pause.)*

Three thousand dollars.

SAM. Holy shit, Leo. Leo, that's...

LEO. *(Freaking out.)* I know

I know

I know

SAM. So what are you gonna do?

LEO. I don't know! I called, I texted – I mean, That's EVERYTHING I had. EVERYTHING! How am I gonna live? How am I gonna pay YOU next month's rent.

    (There's a pause.)

SAM. Well.

I mean, Leo.

I.

I already rented out the room.

LEO. Wait, but I thought you were living alone.

SAM. I just. Financially it makes more sense to get a roommate.

LEO. Even with the advance?

SAM. I mean, I don't even know how much it will be... so...

    *(**LEO** is despondent.)*

LEO. What am I gonna fucking do?

I'm fucked.

I'm fucked.

I'm fucked.

    (He breaks down again.)

SAM. I'm sorry.

And just.

It's been so hard lately. We've been so.

LEO. Sam!

I don't know what I've been thinking! I don't know where I've been.

I just.

I guess I was jealous.

The book. Your agent.

I just didn't know how to.

But you were right all along. You were right about her.

If she was a real friend, she would NEVER leave me high and dry and out three thousand dollars. She would never do that.

You would never do that!

SAM. Of course not. Never.

> *(Pause.)*

(Wracking her brain.) It's so weird. Just up and leaving like that.

I mean MAYBE I did say something that night...

LEO. But Sam!

Like you said WHAT could you have even said that would make her quit?

And ghost me like this? There's nothing you could even say that justifies that!

I don't care. I don't care if you told her to light herself on fire!

SAM. Leo –

LEO. I don't care if you told her you wish her fucking MOM had had an abortion!

SAM. *(This is like, slightly funny to her.)* Leo!

LEO. *(Almost sweetly.)* I mean it. I don't care what you said.

Sheisdeadtome.Fuckingdead.SHE'SFUCKINGDEAD!

Sam. I know things have been strained.

I know I can be difficult. I'm not easy.

And sometimes. How much I need you scares me.

And I need to need you less.

And sometimes that can look a lot like rage.

Or meanness.

Or indifference.

I'm sorry we've had such a hard year.

I promise to be better. I promise.

But Sam, you're it. No question.

You're my fucking best friend. Always.

I'm so sorry I lost sight of that for even a second.

> *(He embraces her fervently. She lets him. She thinks for a long moment. Should she say something?)*

SAM. Hey. You know?

This new subletter.

Maybe I could see if I can get out of it.

LEO. What? Really?

SAM. Yeah, I mean. Who the fuck are they?

They haven't given me a deposit yet. I can back out on them.

LEO. Holy shit, really?

SAM. Yeah, I can tell them it's off.

LEO. Oh my god, Sam. That would save my LIFE. You would be SAVING my life.

SAM. Leo, you're my person. I can't have you be homeless. How would that make ME look?

(He smiles. He hugs her again.)

LEO. But. I mean...without that three grand. I don't know when I'll be able to pay rent again.

SAM. Please, you barely paid rent / before

LEO. / I'm serious. I am really fucked.

SAM. I'll use my advance when it comes in. It'll probably be enough to cover it. If Lola can get one hundred and fifty K, surely I'll get at least fifteen, even with my shitty luck.

LEO. Sam, I can't ask you to do that.

SAM. You didn't ask.

LEO. That's too much. What about getting rid of some day jobs?

SAM. It probably won't be enough to do that anyway.

LEO. Sam. Three grand. That's too much.

SAM. *(Simply.)* You're worth it.

LEO. *(Getting emotional.)* Oh, Sam. So are you. You're worth one million bucks.

SAM. You promise? Because for a minute there, it looked like you were about to trade me in.

Like you were gonna choose some Romper-ass bitch over me.

LEO. And break up Team Fat/Gay?

SAM. I'm fat, you're gay.

LEO. I would never.

We have something she will never have because she has NEVER fucking struggled.

We have ideas. We are fucking survivors.

Together we're limitless.

> *(***LEO*** *embraces her.* ***SAM****'s expression is a little inscrutable.)*

Later. Perhaps six months. Perhaps a year.

> (**LEO** *sits alone.* **SAM** *enters. She's got a paper takeout bag and she kicks off her shoes.*)

SAM. I made it to the Indian place before they closed.

I got veggie samosas and the extra green sauce because you have the palate of a small child –

> (**LEO** *looks at her like he's seen a ghost.*)

(*Advancing to him.*) Hey, everything okay –

> (**LEO** *stands up, backing away from her.*)

Leo, what's –

> (*A door opens [the bathroom].* **SAM** *looks towards it.* **CHLOE**.)

CHLOE. Hi Sam.

SAM. Leo, what is this? Why –

CHLOE. Sam. I told him.

SAM. Told him what?

CHLOE. Everything.

SAM. (*Still trying, performing for* **LEO**.) You mean...Why you just up and ghosted and didn't even have the –

CHLOE. Sam. Stop. It's over.

SAM. I don't know what you're talking about.

CHLOE. (*Almost pitying.*) I told him what you did.

> (**LEO** *looks up at her. She's caught.*)

SAM. (*Starting to panic a little, to* **CHLOE**.) We had a deal.

CHLOE. I know. I came to give you your money back. I don't want it. I'm sorry I ever took it.

SAM. Leo, don't listen to her. She's a liar.

CHLOE. *(Still feeling bad for her, in a way.)* Sam.

You know that isn't true.

> *(She fishes out a check. Attempts to hand it to **SAM**, who does not take it. Fine, then. **CHLOE** then leaves it near **SAM** and turns back to **LEO**. This is why she came. She has to make amends with him.)*

*(To **LEO**.)* Leo. I really am sorry.

This is the worst thing I've ever done.

I don't expect you to forgive me.

But I swear, it's been tearing me apart for six months.

> *(She waits for **LEO** to say something. He doesn't. She goes on. **SAM** is terrified, like watching a car accident you can't stop, is there any way out of this? Oh god oh god oh god...)*

(Rambling.) I just, I wanted to finish my novel so badly.

And it was. It was just *so much money.*

I would have given it back sooner but without the job I couldn't afford to until now.

Even though I saved every penny.

But then my grandfather died and his life insurance covered the money I'd already spent and –

Sorry.

I just.

I wanted to make this right.

Because I know that no amount of money is worth losing a friend over.

CHLOE. None.

I know / that and –

SAM. *(A rageful last ditch attempt to tarnish **CHLOE**, way too late.)* / Oh please, he was just some fucking fag in the office to you, / you took that money the SECOND I offered it –

CHLOE. *(Turning on her, How dare she!)* / I know you think my life is easy, Sam; I know you think I'm basic.

> *(But then. **CHLOE** is a good person. She does have empathy. She knows that's why she can feel sorry for **SAM**. Who, in her mind, has none.)*

But I know how to play a role. I'm a woman, too.

And since the moment I met you, you've cast me as the villain.

So I let you. To get along. To fill the void. To be the thing that was needed.

I'm good at giving people what they want.

The problem is, I've never actually been the enemy here.

No matter how hard you tried to make me.

Because with my friends? I usually just get brunch.

Sometimes there's a BABY SHOWER.

I don't play in the big leagues like you.

> *(She looks over to **LEO**.)*

Leo, I'd still really like to be your friend someday.

If you can ever forgive me.

> *(She starts to go.)*

CHLOE. Sam.

I really hope you get some fucking help.

(She's gone. A deadly silence.)

SAM. Leo –

LEO. How much money did you give her to cut me off?

SAM. It doesn't matter.

LEO. HOW MUCH DID YOU PAY HER?

(Pause.)

SAM. One hundred thousand dollars.

(Silence.)

LEO. From –

SAM. The advance, yes.

(Silence.)

LEO. Guess you got your happy meal after all.

SAM. Leo –

LEO. You could have quit every / job. You could have –

SAM. *(Inarticulately.)* / The money isn't everything, you are.

LEO. *I* am??? I *AM?!*

You let me think.

For *months*. You let me think she had...

You watched me *suffer* and you never said *anything*.

I went to therapy. I was out of my mind.

SAM. I love you.

I love you so much.

SAM. This was our last hope.

   I did it for us.

LEO. Us? You sound fucking insane?

SAM. *(She breaks.)* I know I know I know I know *(You can have as many of these as you want, or as few.)*

   But I could feel you pulling away and –

   I could tell you were going to leave. You were moving and I. I had to...Make you hate *her*.

LEO. Sam. That's.

> *(There's a silence. Goes to his room. We hear some shuffling. **SAM** holds her hands over her mouth as if to stifle a scream. But after a moment **LEO** returns with a bag.)*

SAM. Leo. Please. Where are you going?

LEO. I've been trying to grow up for so long, and now I see why I couldn't.

   It's a relief in a way.

   To know it was never all my fault.

SAM. *(Trying to pull it together.)* Leo. Please. I know I seem crazy. But It's me. It's still me. It's us. I know we can fix this. We can *always* find a way back.

LEO. *(Trying to give her a gift.)* Sam. I have always, always believed that you are special.

   You are fucking amazing.

   And I really I hope you find what you're looking for.

   I'm fucking terrified what will happen if you don't.

> *(**LEO** exits. **SAM** is alone.)*

> *(Lights. Perhaps this transition is longer than the others. Perhaps.)*

Five Years Later

> (**LEO** *is in a nice, sexy suit. He stands
> holding a drink. This is a wedding. A song
> in the style of "Linger" by The Cranberries is
> playing.* He watches the dance floor.* **SAM**
> *approaches, dressed up. Perhaps, maybe
> perhaps in an outfit resembling...ever so
> slightly...high drag.)*

SAM. Hey stranger...

LEO. Hey.

SAM. Saw you hanging on your own over here. Thought
I'd come say hi.

LEO. Hi.

SAM. You were eyeing me across the room.

LEO. I would never.

> *(Pause.)*

Yes I was.

> *(Pause.)*

You look good.

SAM. Thanks. As always, you look like shit.

---

* A license to produce the play *I Wanna Fucking Tear You Apart* does not
include a performance license for the song "Linger." The publisher and
author suggest that the licensee contact ASCAP or BMI to ascertain the
music publisher and contact such music publisher to license or acquire
permission for performance of the song. If a license or permission
is unattainable for "Linger" the licensee may not use the song in the
play *I Wanna Fucking Tear You Apart* but should create an original
composition in a similar style or use a similar song in the public domain.
For further information, please see the Music and Third-Party Materials
Use Note on page iii.

(Pause.)

LEO. Ran into Mike at the buffet.

SAM. Oh yeah?

LEO. ...the tux really masks the *(He gestures to his crotch.)*

SAM. *(Laughing.)* Oh my god, you're the worst. I told you, it's even more sensitive than reg–

LEO. Thank God. Thank God.

(She smiles.)

SAM. How have you been?

LEO. Good. Good.

And you!...Emily told me about –

SAM. *(Holds up her hand.)* Yup. Who would have thought it? This fat fucking cunt.

LEO. *(Seriously.)* I would have.

(Pause.)

SAM. I could pretend I don't know what you're up to. But like. Social media stalking.

LEO. Haha yeah...yeah...it's fun, I like it. Weirdly. I like it a lot.

SAM. I bet you're amazing at it. I would have died to have you as my English teacher. Oh my god. I bet you're so cute with all the dorks who have lunch in your office.

LEO. Totally. And as an added bonus, get to stand up there every day, an unwavering political message to the fats and the gays – "you too can be a boring adult!"

SAM. Oh come on, you love it. You love being adored.

LEO. It's part of my charm.

(Pause.)

SAM. *(With a smug grin.)* Did you see the...did you see the –

LEO & SAM. Cupcake Tower.

LEO. Oh my god, I couldn't even look at you.

SAM.	**LEO**.
Whole piece of cake. WHOLE piece.	At a gay wedding. I would have expected more.

    (Pause.)

SAM. I wanted to say I'm sorry for. Well. Gee, where to begin. /

LEO. / It's okay. I forgive you. It feels like a lifetime ago now.

SAM. It does and it doesn't to me.

LEO. ...

    I read your new book. I read it twice.

    It's amazing.

       *(**SAM** starts to cry, maybe.)*

    You did it all on your own.

SAM. I did.

LEO. I'm proud of you.

SAM. Thank you.

       (The music changes. It's quiet. They don't notice.)

LEO. It's hard to know what to say to you.

    It feels weird not to know.

SAM. It does.

       (Pause.)

LEO. Mike is probably looking for you.

SAM. Eh. It's fine.

He knows he's sixth.

> *(The music gets loud enough that they hear it.* **LEO** *gestures to the air, like "hear that?" It plays on...the end of the song.)*

> *(She holds out her hand to him.)*

> *(Their chemistry.)*

> *(It was always undeniable.)*

> *(As the song's final chorus plays,* **SAM** *and* **LEO** *start to dance, it's a little goofy and awkward at first, then it finds itself. If you are playing She Wants Revenge's "I Wanna Fucking Tear You Apart," we might hear the final line of the song as* **SAM** *and* **LEO** *embrace fiercely, ferociously.* * *A goodbye forever.)*

> *(Blackout.)*

---

* A license to produce the play *I Wanna Fucking Tear You Apart* does not include a performance license for the song "I Wanna Fucking Tear You Apart." The publisher and author suggest that the licensee contact ASCAP or BMI to ascertain the music publisher and contact such music publisher to license or acquire permission for performance of the song. If a license or permission is unattainable for "I Wanna Fucking Tear You Apart," the licensee may not use the song in the play *I Wanna Fucking Tear You Apart* but should create an original composition in a similar style or use a similar song in the public domain. For further information, please see the Music and Third-Party Materials Use Note on page iii.

THE SECTION IN JANUARY IF LEO IS PLAYED BY AN ACTOR OF COLOR...

(They start to eat.)

LEO. I solved gentrification.

SAM. Gentrification. In general?

LEO. Yeah, well, you know how like, everyone has been trying to think of a way to fix that?

SAM. I do. I. Do.

LEO. Well, I know this sounds nuts, but like. I figured it out.

SAM. Please. Enlighten me.

LEO. You're being snide. I can tell you're being snide.

SAM. It's just. You know. The greatest minds of our time... urban planners. Politicians. Social Justice Warriors /

LEO. Ugh, that term –

SAM. For like, the past thousand years couldn't figure this out. But one visit to Pret A Manger and you've come up with it? Forgive my small doubt.

LEO. Okay, but you have to admit I'm pretty political. I'm up on politics. / You've even said so.

SAM. / Is this politics, though?

LEO. Seriously. Remember when I explained trickle down economics to you?

SAM. Yes.

LEO. So like. It's not totally out there that I could actually have the solution.

SAM. Okay, okay. I'm all ears. Lay it on me.

LEO. Okay so the big issue is that people in neighborhoods of color are getting pushed out because white people want cheaper housing.

SAM. Sure.

LEO. But like. We need to figure out a way to keep white people out of historically black and brown neighborhoods. And keep white people in white neighborhoods.

SAM. Uhhhhhhhhh

LEO. But honestly, a lot of white people – due to the legitimately SKYROCKETING rent prices – they struggle to pay too.

SAM. Mmm...yes...

LEO. So! What we should do is like subsidize housing in WHITE neighborhoods.

SAM. Are you actually suggesting giving more money to white people?

LEO. No no no no no of COURSE not that would be ridiculous.

SAM. Right.

LEO. I'm suggesting giving money to the *landlords* of the white buildings...you know, not all of the *landlords* are white...it's not about race –

SAM. It is.

LEO. No but like, I mean, I'm Mexican.* My family is *directly* impacted by this.

SAM. Oh, no I know.

But –

---

* "Mexican" can be replaced with the ethnicity of the actor playing Leo.

LEO. And like, we deserve some protection from white people taking our neighborhoods. But it's gross and white savior-y to pay for OUR housing. So like...we should just pay to keep the white people where they belong.

SAM. Okay, okay...let's skip over the "where they belong" thought – because, like yikes – but who is "we"?

LEO. Come again?

SAM. The "we" who pays. Who is we?

LEO. Us. Taxes. The government.

SAM. Okay. Is it taxes or the government?

LEO. It's taxes the government USES to pay it.

SAM. So we pay taxes to pay the white people / to

LEO. The landlords the white LANDLORDS

SAM. Okay, the *landlords*, to keep the white people in their neighborhoods.

LEO. Yes.

SAM. But like, EVERYONE pays taxes. So we'd be raising taxes for EVERYONE. Including people of color.

LEO. I guess.

SAM. So people of color would actually be paying the rents of white people on top of their own.

LEO. I mean...

SAM. And...it has to be said. Who decides what a "white" neighborhood is and what a "non-white" neighborhood is? Like who is on the zoning committee to make these decisions? A bunch of white people?

LEO. That would probably have to get figured out, yes.

SAM. So wouldn't that all be even WORSE than gentrification now? Or at least the same?

LEO. Mmmm.

SAM. So. I kind of think that your solution works in theory, but in practice. In practice it might have some flaws.

LEO. Well, I mean I only thought about it for like fifteen minutes.

SAM. Sure.

LEO. But like, I think the basis for my logic was pretty good.

SAM. No it was. It was.

LEO. Yeah.

(*Pause. He checks his phone.*)

www.ingramcontent.com/pod-product-compliance
Lightning Source LLC
Chambersburg PA
CBHW070336120726
47909CB00008B/2705